HITTITE WARRIOR

Also by Joanne Williamson

Jacobin's Daughter
The Eagles Have Flown
The Glorious Conspiracy
God King
The Iron Charm
And Forever Free
To Dream Upon a Crown

HITTITE WARRIOR

BETHLEHEM BOOKS • IGNATIUS PRESS
BATHGATE, N.D. SAN FRANCISCO

Originally published by Alfred Knopf, 1960

Cover and map design by Davin Carlson

Title page illustration by John Herreid

First Bethlehem Books printing, April 1999

ISBN 978–1–883937–38–6
LCCN: 98-73485

Bethlehem Books • Ignatius Press
10194 Garfield Street South
Bathgate, ND 58216
1-800-757-6831
www.bethlehembooks.com

Printed in the United States on acid free paper

Manufactured by Thomson-Shore, Dexter, MI (USA); RMA589LS205, March, 2013

Contents

Introduction

THE KEY TO making history memorable and exciting to young people is to make it real for them. Bringing the historical period and its significant people and events to life, turns what would otherwise be a dull rote lesson into living information about real people and happenings, which everyone loves. Those who truly enjoy history talk about it as if the events they were discussing were happening now, as though the important people involved in history were their neighbors.

Joanne Williamson achieves this sense of immediacy in *Hittite Warrior* and encourages the reader's interest in the characters and their lives. Weaving into the narrative a great deal of accurate historical information, she gives a word picture of important events, geography, and interactions among the nations during the 12th century before Christ, when the prophetess Deborah was judge in Israel. And, she makes it all an exciting, well-told tale.

We see in the course of the story what living conditions were like for the Hittites, Canaanites, and the Jewish People at this period of history. Uriah, a Hittite youth, is driven from his home by the Achaeans (the Greeks), given succor by a Canaanite boy and his family, sheltered by the Israelites (Jews), forced to fight with the Canaanites against the Jews, and finally received by the Israelites as a scribe.

To make connections in time and space is an important aspect of good historical fiction, and *Hittite Warrior* well succeeds in doing this for a time period that is unknown and unclear to most people. It also performs another great service as a vehicle for allowing children to see history as the unfolding of God's plan.

There is a temptation to separate our study of God's plan for the Jews, his Chosen People, from the ordinary study of ancient civilizations. For one thing, most modern texts compartmentalize the various ancient peoples. Egypt is studied, then Babylonia, then Greece, then Rome. The tie between these cultures is largely seen as simply chronological; one came before or after the others. But there is a more important relation between all cultures. They are all moving toward or away from the central historical event of all time: the incarnation of the Son of God. *Hittite Warrior* makes clear the connection of salvation history with the rest of the events of the world. For this reason it is a very important book, and one more reason to be grateful to Bethlehem Books.

A WORD TO THE HOME EDUCATOR

It is essential to an excellent education that good literature be a significant component of the curriculum. This literature should, first and foremost, be enjoyed. I am opposed to breaking up an interesting story to insert lessons. Such a procedure destroys the inherent unity of the narrative. However, once the story is read, going back to interesting or important sections to discuss or summarize can bring out truths that the student may have missed, or highlight peripheral information that is worth following up on. It can also be a way to encourage writing and summarizing skills.

The younger child can be asked to retell, first orally, and then in writing, his favorite event from the story. If writing is a chore, write down his retelling, and let him copy it later, thus separating composition from the physical act of writing.

Older students can be encouraged, after reading the text, to pick out the single most important event in the story. This will probably lead to a discussion of what constitutes "important." Most important to the characters, as they see the events unfold? Or most important as seen with the clarity of hindsight? Or most important to the reader, who is in a privileged position relative to the events? Finally, this last sense of important seems most significant, but the student can be encouraged to analyze the various senses of the word and draw a conclusion. Once he determines what is most important, he may be asked to do two things (not on the same day). First ask him to retell this event in his own words, in writing, and later ask him to summarize the event. This gives him a chance to think about the difference between retelling and summarizing, an important consideration.

Then the student could be asked what he thinks is the most interesting event in the story. Is it the same as the most important? Perhaps in one sense, but not in another. Or maybe they coincide. These are the kinds of questions that will awaken the analytic powers of the student. Have him think about the question and draw a conclusion, and communicate his conclusion to you, giving reasons for it. This process, at this point of intellectual formation, is more important than "getting the right answer."

It would be useful for the student, whatever his age, to track the events of the story on a map. A map which the student has produced himself, even by tracing it, is always more productive, because it involves more of his attention to the details of the map. A clearer picture of the events emerges as the movements of the characters are followed geographically, and the relations between the various peoples encountered in the story becomes clearer as well.

Similarly, a timeline is useful in the effort to maintain the integration of salvation history with the events that are less clearly related to God's plan for our redemption.

Additionally, after these activities, a reading of Judges, Chapter 4, would provide more opportunities for comparison and a better understanding of the events of Scripture.

All of these suggestions for teaching history will be more fruitful if there is discussion between you and your child. It is in such discussions that the opportunity for the best formation, the formation concerning principles, occurs.

Laura M. Berquist
Ojai, California
February, 1999

Hittite Warrior

"The kings came and fought,
then fought the kings of Canaan . . .
The river of Kishon swept them away . . ."

The Song of Deborah

This story, based on an episode in the Bible's Book of Judges, took place about 200 years before the days of Saul and David, and about 1200 before the birth of Christ.

GREECE
Troy
Mycenae
HITTIT
MINOAN-MYCENAEAN
CRETE
Knossos
CYP
Mediterranean
Sea
Memphis
0 50 100 200 300
MILES

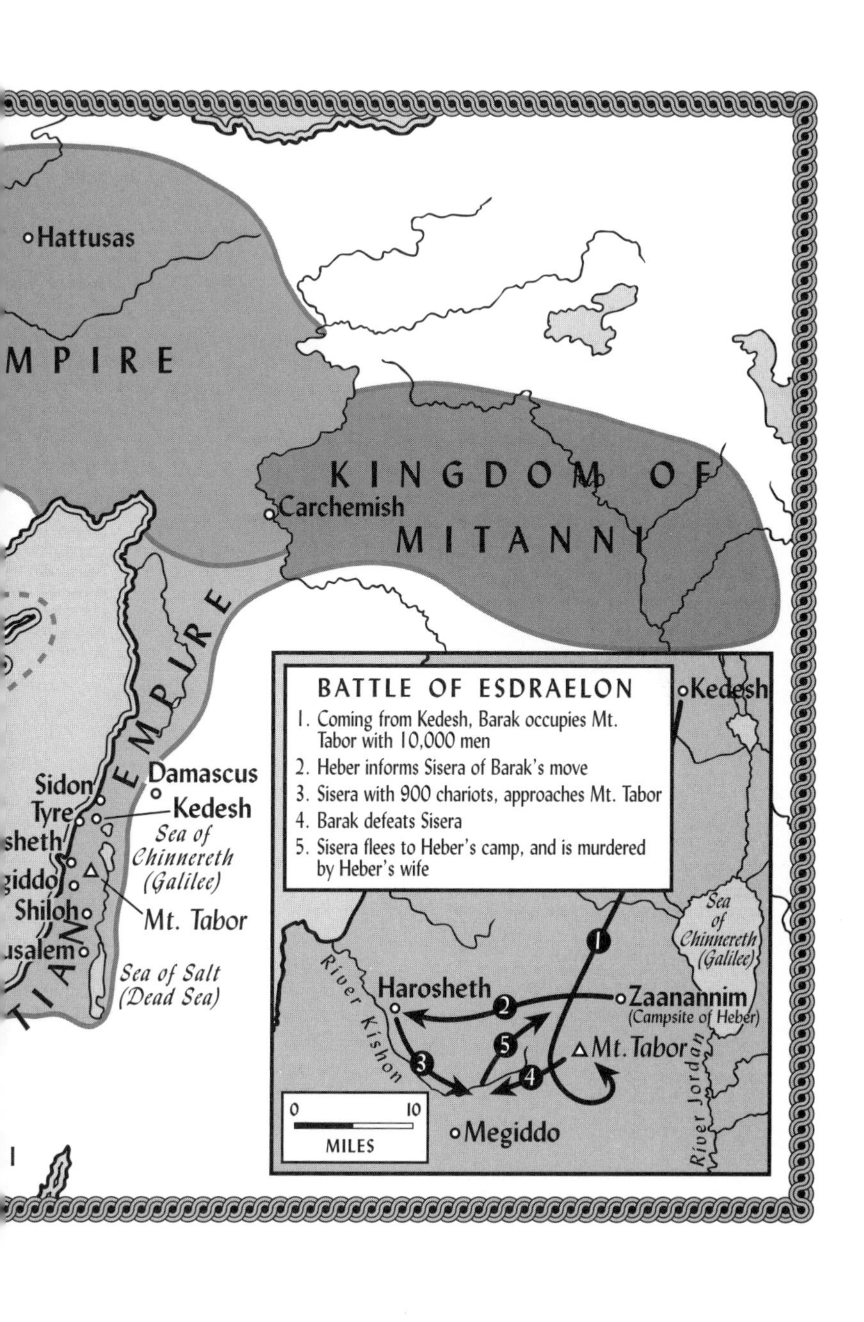
Hattusas
KINGDOM OF
MITANNI
Carchemish
EMPIRE
Damascus
Sidon
Tyre
Kedesh
Sea of Chinnereth (Galilee)
Shiloh
Mt. Tabor
Sea of Salt (Dead Sea)
BATTLE OF ESDRAELON
1. Coming from Kedesh, Barak occupies Mt. Tabor with 10,000 men
2. Heber informs Sisera of Barak's move
3. Sisera with 900 chariots, approaches Mt. Tabor
4. Barak defeats Sisera
5. Sisera flees to Heber's camp, and is murdered by Heber's wife
Kedesh
Sea of Chinnereth (Galilee)
Harosheth
Zaanannim
(Campsite of Heber)
Mt. Tabor
River Kishon
River Jordan
Megiddo
0
10
MILES

« prologue »
Introducing a Hittite

I, URIAH-TARHUND, son of Arnandash the horse breeder, am a Hittite. I was born of a race of men who came down from the unknown north a thousand years ago and became the rulers of half the world. But that world has come to an end, and I can never go home again.

I was born in the Hittite province of Arzawa. My father was a kinsman of the chief of the province and raised horses in the grasslands to draw the battle chariots for which our land of Great Hatti was famed.

When I was a child, the world was as it had always been, or so I thought. We, the Hittites, lived in Great Hatti with its rocky mountains, its plains and its forests, stretching to the Black Sea of the north and the great sea of the west. We ruled the northern world; and Egypt, the accursed land, ruled the world of the south.

Other people did not matter. There were the lands of Canaan and the Amorites to the south, with their rich trading cities, divided between us and Egypt. To the east, the lands of Hurri and Mitanni sent us tribute; and sometimes traders from the great city of Babylon came to our towns and villages, but I never spoke to them.

For the nobles of Great Hatti, whose ancestors came down from the northern wilderness a thousand years ago, scorned all merchants and scribes and left such work to the dark skinned, ancient peoples of the land, who had lived there since the world began. Our women, like my mother and my sister Annitis, were kept close at home to guard them from these people; and I myself was not allowed to speak even to the elders of the ancient village where we lived. It was so wherever our fair skinned ancestors had settled and conquered . . . even, the story tellers said, in the far off Hindus valley.

The world was as it had always been, and it was protected by the gods. We Hittites worshipped all the gods, some of them our own, brought with us from the unknown north; many of them the gods of the people with whom we traded or who sent us tribute. We worshipped them all, and we knew that they would always keep us safe and strong.

But they did not. My story will tell of how they failed us, how disaster came upon us all, and how strangely I have survived it. It will tell of the rise and fall of nations, the fading of old glories and the birth of new. And it will tell much of that little strip of land called Canaan to the south, between us and the accursed land of Egypt, which was only a name to me when I was a child. For all the wealth and all the armies and all the glories of the nations have passed through that little land and probably always will; and the story of the kings of Canaan is the story of the world.

« 1 »

The Sea People

I BEGIN MY story with the day I was thirteen years old, the day my father told me I must give up the great horse, Labarnash.

Labarnash was the best horse we ever bred. My father had bought the mare who gave him birth from a trader who had gotten her from the lands around the southern desert. The horses there are larger, more slender, and swifter than our small stocky horses of the north; and Labarnash showed his greatness in his large, well set out eyes and longer ears, his sloping shoulders and round ribs, and his dark gold color.

He was to have been my horse, and I had named him with the titles of the old kings of Hatti, meaning "Great One." I had been in the stable when his mother had first given him birth, and it was I who first saw him stagger onto his long, wobbly legs.

My father had given me full charge of his training and promised that if I handled him well, he would give him to me for my own. So it was I who first haltered him; who first fed him grain; who cared for his hoofs, who combed his mane and tail and groomed him with my own fingers. And it was I who, a year after his birth, first harnessed him beside his mother to a light chariot and drove him out across the steppes.

But now my father had broken his promise. He saw the wonder and reproach in my eyes as I stood before him, my hand on Labarnash's neck, and he tried to make me understand.

"It is the thirteenth year of the reign of the king," he said, "and thirteen is a holy number. All loyal vassals must offer tribute, the best they have to give, and Labarnash is our best. And Uriah, there is more."

He drew me closer to him and spoke slowly, as if to give his words more weight.

"I have kept these things from your mother and sister," he said to me. "But you are a man now, and may know the truth. There is trouble in the land of Hatti. Do you remember the stories of the rebel chief, Maduwattas?"

I shivered. Every child knew the stories that were told of Maduwattas. For many years there had been a shadow across our world. Out across the western sea lived the men we called the sea people, whose great island was Crete and whose great city was Mycenae on the western mainland. They called themselves Achaeans. Their princes were sometimes sent to Hattusas, our great city, to learn the arts of chariots and horsemanship, and they had become jealous of our lands and power.

In the years when my father was a child, a Hittite traitor called Maduwattas had sold himself to Atreus, an Achaean chief, and had come raiding and burning into the province of Arzawa. Some of the old Arzawans, who hated their Hittite masters, had joined him and a time of terror had come upon the land that had never been forgotten.

"But Maduwattas has been dead for many years," I said. "And Atreus the Achaean must be a very old man."

"Their spirit is still alive," said my father. "Rumors have come to us from the north of strange tribes from over the border who are bringing terror upon the people there. And even here in the south strange sights have been seen and strange stories are being told. There are those who say that such trouble is coming upon the land as has never been seen before, and that the hand of the king is not as strong upon the country as it has been before. He did not make the holy pilgrimage this year, to lead the worship of the gods of the provinces." He stared before him a moment, then smiled and laid his hand on my shoulder. "You see why we must all prove our loyalty and our faith in this holy year."

"I understand," I said at last, though my hand tightened on the mane of Labarnash.

"Good," said my father. "Then tomorrow we will go to Haballa and find a caravan to take us to Hattusas."

"Hattusas?" I cried. "The great city?"

"Yes," said my father, pleased that my spirits had been raised. "There will be a great pilgrimage and great celebrations. If our king will not come to us, we will go to him."

And for a moment I almost forgot my grief over Labarnash in my excitement over the journey we were to make. For I had never been to Hattusas, or to any town except Haballa, for the horse fairs.

My father told the servants of our plans for the journey and gave strict orders for the guarding of our house and lands. He commanded all the men of the household to keep themselves well armed. For my mother and sister, being women, were to be left behind.

"If I were an Egyptian woman I would be allowed to go," said my sister Annitis bitterly, and my mother frowned at the name of the accursed land.

"Women in Egypt are as evil as the men," she said.

My father watched them with troubled eyes. And once, during that last night before the journey, I thought he had changed his mind. Then he shook his head as if in anger.

"I will not stay at home in fear in this holy year," he said, "because of rumors and old women's stories. There are people in Arzawa who have always hated the king of Hatti. It is they who are trying to spread fear among those of us who are loyal. Still, I could wish that Hattusas were nearer home."

I was not worried. "Nothing could happen to Mother and Annitis," I told my father. "The gods will protect us all."

And so we joined a caravan, my father and I, for the journey to the great city.

It was a journey of many days through grasslands, hills, valleys, and later the rocky mountainous lands of the north. For Hattusas lay in its mountains like the nest of a giant bird. A robbers' retreat, the Egyptians called it. My heart still beats faster as I remember the road that led to it marked, as we neared the city, by giant images in stone . . . lions for the holy goddess of Arinna, bulls for Teshub, god of thunder, god of the double axe. To reach the city, we had to ford a great river, which I did not like; for I was afraid of water.

"Will it be as big as Haballa?" I asked my father. "Will there be a fair with jugglers and fire eaters? I wish it were time for the winter festival. I would like to see that play of the god slaying the dragon again."

My father laughed.

"Once you have seen Hattusas," he said, "all others, even Haballa, will be as mud villages in your eyes."

And it was true. The first sight of the great, rock-hewn wall of the city struck awe into my heart. The gateways and buildings of solid stone were such as I had never seen before; and I was so taken up with the great sights that I forgot that we must leave

Labarnash in the stables of the king until the moment was upon us; and, for the first time, I realized that I would probably never see him again.

If I had been alone, I would have thrown my arms around his proud neck and wept and kissed him. But I was not alone, and could only watch while they took him away . . . Labarnash whom I had raised and come to love, and whom I had named "Great One."

When he had disappeared from sight, I turned to my father in a kind of amazement.

"I will never see him again!" I cried.

"How can you be sure?" said my father. "It is in the hands of the gods."

But I was not comforted. For the first time in my life, I had lost a thing I loved.

That night they held the celebration in honor of the thirteenth year of the reign of the king. My father and I, being related to the great families of Hattusas, were allowed a place in the hall.

I forgot my grief for a while in wonder at all I saw. All the loyal chiefs of great Hatti were there . . . our own noble kinsman, the chief of Arzawa, in fashionably braided hair, pointed shoes, tall hat with upturned brim, earrings and a cane. There were ambassadors from Egypt in pleated kilts and elaborately curled wigs. There was the Dardanian chief Paris Aleksandus, from distant Troy, whose grandfather had fought with us against the second Rameses of Egypt at the battle of Kadesh.

The young prince who would be the second Subiluliuma was with his father the king and, when they stood together on the great stone stairway, all shouted and clashed their wine cups.

"Labarnash! Labarnash!" they cried, meaning "great one." And tears came to my eyes at the thought of my own Labarnash. But my father looked strange and grim; and many there must have known in their hearts that such a sight would never again be seen in Hattusas. For, though we did not know it on that day, the glory of Great Hatti was at an end.

We did not stay long in the great city. Things had become strangely quiet in Hattusas. People spoke little, and my father said it was as if someone had muffled the sounds of the streets with a blanket. On the morning of our departure, a madman ran through the temple square shouting:

"Midas is coming! Midas is coming to destroy us all!"

But two soldiers seized him and dragged him off. I suppose he was killed and hung up by the gates of the city, like other criminals that we had seen there.

"What was he saying?" I asked my father.

"He spoke of Midas the Phrygian," he replied. "A barbarian chief, one of the sea people. There are stories that he has come into the north with his tribe and is laying waste wherever he passes, but the King has forbidden it to be told, for fear of frightening the people. Whether this is true or not, I give thanks that it is still far from Arzawa."

As we passed from the city with the returning caravan, I looked back at the great walls. I am glad I stared at them so long and remember them so well, for I never saw them again.

It was on the road back into Arzawa that we saw it. From a valley some distance away a strange smell reached us and the sight of smoke curling into the air. The master of the caravan was a Babylonian and interested only in the merchandise he was carrying toward the western sea. He would not stop or leave the road to see what the trouble was, or if there were any in need of help.

"Uriah," said my father, "you and I are men of Arzawa and cannot pass by when our brothers may be in distress."

So we left the caravan and rode our sturdy little northern horses as fast as we could toward the strange thing in the valley. Though I have seen many terrible sights since then, I still remember that one.

A village had been burned to the ground along with the land around it. Many men lay dead and dying, and some women and children; though many of these had perhaps fled or been carried off. Only one man was left unharmed, sitting dazed and staring against the stone wall of a half-destroyed hut.

"Who has done this thing?" cried my father, speaking to him as if he had been a brother, though he was only a serf, of the ancient people of the land.

"Maduwattas," replied the man. I shuddered and drew closer to my father.

"Maduwattas is dead," said my father.

"But he has come back," said the man. "And he has brought the sea people with him."

"Surely he is mad, father," I whispered, shuddering again and trying to draw him away.

But my father spoke gently to the man; and soon he began to sob and talk to him, telling him how a great line of ox carts had come into the valley, guarded by armed men in chariots, and carrying women and children and all manner of riches.

"They came from the west," said the man, "and did not speak our language, so they are surely from the sea. The armed men fell upon us and killed us all, except some of our women and children that they took away to serve them. Why did they do it? Our village was not loyal to the King of Hatti."

I knew father ought to kill the man at once for saying that, but was glad when he did not.

"The sea people," said my father softly. "Atreus is old or dead; but his sons are mighty among the Achaeans. They have come into Arzawa, as Midas the Phrygian has come into the north. Come, we will ride for home."

We did not go back to the road or rejoin the caravan, but rode across the country with all speed till we came to our own acres, and found that we had come too late. Our village too had been burned, our home and our land destroyed, and our servants slain.

My father said nothing at the sight, but threw himself from his horse and ran among the bodies and the smoking ruins, searching for some sign of my mother and my sister. I stayed on my horse, for I could not have moved.

But then my father gave a great cry and fell on his knees, and I knew what he had found. I knew that I would never see my mother and my sister Annitis again and that all the world, as I had known it, had been destroyed.

This happened in my fourteenth year. They say that four years later, Hattusas itself was destroyed. The armies came down from the north and the west and from the islands in the western sea, with giant shields and plumed helmets decorated with the tusks of boars. Wives and families followed in ox carts laden with all their possessions . . . precious iron ornaments and dainty gold and silver objects of the old style from Crete and Mycenae. None stood before them. No Dardanians from Troy came to our aid, for Troy had fought for its life and lost, near the shores of the western sea.

For three years after the destruction of our home my father and I lived on in the ruins, making a bare living with our bees and what was left of our orchards and the food we could raise. We could not fight the enemy, for there were none to join us. Those who had not been slain by the sea people were either too terrified to stand against them, or did not care who were their masters, Achaeans or Hittite nobles. We lived as servants of the conquerors, who would come to us at any time and take what they wanted, and strike us down if we did not give it to them soon enough.

One day when I was sixteen, two men drove up in a chariot to where my father and I were gathering in fruit. One was a captain of the sea people, and the other was his servant and charioteer.

"You!" said the captain to my father, as we had spoken to the serfs in the old days. "All that you harvest is confiscated for our chief in Haballa. My driver will stay with you and see that you don't shirk."

My father stood for a moment with his head bowed. Then suddenly he straightened and stared into the eyes of the captain.

"No," he said. And for the first time in three years, he seemed like my father again.

The captain was a tall man with blue eyes and a dark brown beard. His driver was short and dark and powerful. The driver seized my father from behind and held him while the captain struck him across the face, shoulders, and chest with the butt end of his spear.

"The gods destroy you, you dogs!" I shouted, and sprang upon the captain. But a blow from his spear sent me sprawling on the ground, while he finished beating my father. I cried out in agony at every blow he received, but my father made no sound.

Afterward the captain stood back and looked at us in disgust.

"They will do no work today," he said to his driver. "Come. But," he shouted at us over his shoulder, "we will be back."

My father lay on the ground where the driver had let him fall, and at first I thought he was dead. Then I heard him breathing with some difficulty, and I managed to get him into the house, though he cried out with pain at being lifted.

I stayed with him through the day and through the night, but I soon knew that he would not live. He was too badly hurt, too many bones had been broken and he was too weak and tired to fight against death.

"Don't die," I begged him. "Everything is gone. Not you, too."

But he shook his head. "You must not stay here," he said at last. "Promise me."

"Where can I go?" I asked him. "This is my home."

"Not now," he said. "It is *their* home now." He was silent for a time, summoning his strength. "You must go south," he said after a while.

"Where south, Father?" I asked softly, thinking that if he would keep talking, he would not die.

"To the land of Canaan. There is a town. A town called Harosheth. There is a man there."

"What man, Father?"

"A man . . . called Sisera. He will help you. For my sake."

"But what is he to you, Father? And how can I find him?"

"Promise," said my father. And, seeing that he could say no more, I gave my promise.

He did not speak again, and I saw that he was really dying. I clung to him, trying to hold him back from death, but it was no use.

He died. As the holy laws prescribed, I burned his body on a great pyre and mourned him for thirteen days; though there was no Old Woman to come from the village and say the magic rites over his body, nor had I oil or a silver jar in which to lay his bones, nor beer or wine to quench his funeral fire. But no man was ever better mourned.

And when the thirteen days were up, I made my way to Haballa and prepared myself for the long journey into the land of Canaan.

« 2 »

The Merchant from Tyre

CANAAN WAS ONLY a name to me, like its neighboring land of the Amorites. Not too long ago, as the years are counted, we of Great Hatti conquered and possessed all those lands to the south, though Egypt had claimed them. And we and the accursed land had fought for them over the years till the battle of Kadesh, when the boundaries were finally settled. After that, we had ruled the northern lands of Canaan, while Egypt had ruled in the south below the town of Damascus, and there had been an uneasy peace between us.

Harosheth, I knew, was in that part of Canaan ruled by Egypt, and I shuddered to think what might await me there. For all Hittites knew that only evil could come out of Egypt, and that all Egyptians were cruel and treacherous beyond belief. Besides, all Hittites knew that the Canaanites themselves were cowardly and dishonorable men, who set lowly merchants above honest warriors and who taught their children to read and keep accounts instead of fighting for what they wanted. But my father had said that I was to go to Harosheth, and I had given him my promise.

I thought that I would never get to Canaan in any case, no matter what I had promised. For I had no money and little food to last me on the journey. I must travel on foot, for no horses or donkeys had been left to us at home.

I found a caravan, made up of traders from Canaan, who bowed and smiled at the new Achaean masters of Haballa, as they had smiled and bowed to my father before. But we Hittites were no longer their masters. Now they shouted at me and thrust me aside when I tried to speak to them, for I was shabby and poor and one of a conquered race; so I could not find out where in Canaan they were going. But I could not stay in Haballa. So I kept as close to the men of the caravan as I could and, as they left the town, followed in their shadow.

I remember little of those first days of the journey. The road was hot, stony and dusty, and it burned and bruised my feet. The sun grew stronger and crueller as we moved southward, so that I was often dizzy and always thirsty.

There was water for all; but my small supply of food was growing smaller and, though I ate as little as I could, I knew that it would soon be gone and that I would be left to die like a beggar. My thoughts often wandered; and sometimes it seemed that I had been walking along that highway all my life, though I could not tell where or why.

It was on the fourth night that the robbers came down upon us. We had halted for the night at a caravansary along the way. The merchants and their servants had crowded themselves into the dark, bare building that surrounded the courtyard where their supplies and merchandise were loaded. But I stretched myself in the open, preferring the company of the animals and the stars. For, if the Canaanite merchants held me in scorn, I returned the feeling with all the strength I had left.

I lay on the ground in my threadbare robe, listening to the soft sounds made by the beasts . . . donkeys, mostly, and goats brought along for their milk. There were no horses. The traders in this caravan rode on donkeys or, if they were rich enough, in sedan chairs carried by servants.

I thought with longing of the horses I had known at home. I remembered other nights when I had slept in the open with the young colts, with Labarnash.

"Labarnash!" I whispered. "Where are you now?" But I thought that he was probably dead.

The moon was bright, but there were shadows all around me. If my ears had not been dulled by hunger and weakness, I would have heard the sound before; but I did not hear it till the new shadow fell across me.

I turned my head and looked up into a dirty, brown, bearded face. It was twisted and ugly. At the same time that I saw it, I saw that a hand was raised above me and that there was a knife in it.

I rolled aside and the knife came down on the spot where I had been an instant before. As the man sprawled in surprise, I gathered myself together and sprang upon him.

I was sick from weariness and lack of food; and I would never have been so strong if all the rage of the past three years had not come upon me. I wanted to kill this strange man because, if I did not, I knew he would kill me; but also because the sea people had killed my mother and sister, destroyed my home, and beaten my father to death; and because the Canaanite merchants no longer bowed to me, but pushed me aside and treated me like a serf. So I fell upon him from behind, seized him by the wrists and twisted his arms behind him till he screamed and the knife fell from his hand. Then we both struggled for it on the ground, and I was the one who got it. He tried to force it from me; but he, being a robber, was probably not much stronger or better nourished than I was, and I was so full of hate that it served me better than a well-fed body. So I broke his grip, threw him to the ground, then fell upon him again and plunged his own knife into him till he was dead.

There had been wild men like this one at home, who would rob and kill when they could; so I knew that he was probably a lookout sent on ahead of his band to see if the men of the caravan were asleep, and to kill any guards. I knew the other bandits had probably heard his scream and would soon be down upon us. So, when I saw that he was safely dead, I stood up and shouted to those inside the caravansary.

"Hey!" I shouted. "You lazy fat ones in there! Stand up, if you can, and pick up your weapons! Somebody else is after your silver!"

I made a lot of noise and shouted many more unflattering things, enjoying myself for the first time in three years. The merchants had probably heard the scream of the robber, too. So they all came piling out, armed with their staves and their bronze and jeweled daggers. I burst out laughing at the sight of them. They came just in time, however; for, as I expected, the robber band now came pouring down, shrieking fearfully, laying about them with sticks, and shooting stones from slings.

It was not much of a fight. The robbers were poor, simple-minded, hungry men, stupid from starvation. And, though the traders were not very good fighters as we would have counted it in Arzawa, they were well fed, armed and quick witted. So they soon drove them off and sent them howling away into the countryside.

But before they did so, one of the merchants nearly lost his life. He was a young man, who handled his stave fairly well. But one of the robbers got past it and would have cut his throat if I had not seen what was happening. I felt no love for the young merchant, but was not on the side of the robbers, so I came up behind the bandit and struck him a tremendous blow over the head with a stick

I had picked up. So the young man's life was saved, the last robber was sent running off to join his fellows, and peace settled down upon us again.

It had been a great night for me. I thanked the gods for letting me prove myself worthy of my training at home. I had fought well and saved a life, together with much valuable property. Now, if I must be left along the roadside to die, at least I would not die in shame. I fell into a deep, restful sleep.

In the morning, before the caravan set out again, a very dirty donkey boy came to me and said his master wanted to see me. It was the first time any of them had spoken to me except in anger; and, remembering that I was the son of a Hittite lord, I tried to make myself as clean as possible. I even took the trouble to braid my hair. I ate the last of my food supply to give myself strength, then followed the donkey boy to the man who wanted to see me.

It was the young man whose life I had saved. I had noticed him before, for he was one of the magnificent ones who rode in a sedan chair with cushions and carved ivory fittings, carried by four strong men. I had seen such things before only in Hattusas, and very few of them even there.

He was not much older than I and was as handsome as the Canaanite god Adoni, with white teeth and the beginnings of a young beard. He wore a fine, cone-shaped hat, beautifully made sandals and a robe and tunic bordered in the deep, bright purple that had been worn by the royal family in Hattusas.

Besides this, he carried an elegantly carved walking stick. I had tried to hold him in scorn, but could not help admiring him.

"You have done a great thing for me," he said, after staring at me for a little while. "Are you a free born man?"

"My father," I said proudly, "was a lord and a kinsman of the chief of the province of Arzawa." And you, I added to myself, are nothing but a buyer and seller of goods, and your people have never been anything but the slaves of stronger nations.

But the young man could not hear what I said to myself. He smiled a wonderfully bright, sweet smile.

"In that case," he said, "you are as my brother, for you have saved my life. Have you food for the rest of the journey?"

I was ashamed, but told him the truth.

"Then you will share mine," said the young man. And to prove that he meant it, he had his servant bring me a skin of goat's milk, from which I drank heartily, and some honey cakes to go with it.

Never having met anyone like this magnificent person before, I was silent at first, and waited to see what he would say to me.

"My name is Hannibaal ben Ethbaal," he said, when I had finished the milk and cakes. "My father is an Elder of Tyre."

I had heard of Tyre. It was a city on the coast of Canaan, not so big and thriving as Sidon, its neighbor to the north, but a rich, powerful town. Like most of these cities it was ruled by Egypt, but governed by its own chief, high priest, and council of Elders, all chosen from among the great merchant families of the town. Hannibaal, it seemed, was making his first trading journey with this caravan, to practice the arts of buying and selling his father's goods in a foreign land.

"Then this caravan," I said, "is headed for Tyre. Is Harosheth far from Tyre?"

"Harosheth?" Hannibaal frowned in surprise. "What have you to do in Harosheth?"

I told him of my father's death and the reason for my journey into Canaan.

"I am sorry for what happened to your father," said Hannibaal, "though we in Canaan have no reason to love the Hittites. But," he added, "you will find little peace or safety in Harosheth."

"Why not?" I asked him.

"Because it is a hill town," he said, "inland in Canaan. They say it is the fiercest and cruelest town of all. They are rough and lawless there in the hills, and the country is full of robbers and rebels. They fight among themselves, and ten years seldom goes by that one of their cities has not destroyed one of the others. They have not our wealth and trade, you see, so they are not so well protected by Egypt as we are on the coast."

I wondered, if the inland cities were always at war with one another, how I could be sure that my father's friend was still alive.

"All the same," I said, "I must go to Harosheth. I have given my promise."

"You must rest in Tyre first," said Hannibaal. "My father is an honorable man, and he will not let you go without rewarding you for saving my life. Stay close to my supply train, and take what food you need. When we come to Tyre, my servants will guide you to my father's house."

The signal was given for the caravan to set out again. Hannibaal ben Ethbaal was lifted in his chair on the shoulders of his four husky bearers and I stared after him, bewildered and uncertain; then I followed after his supplies and his donkey boys. I could not understand this sudden burst of fortune that had come upon me, and could not really believe that any good could come to me, a Hittite, at the hands of a Canaanite trader. But at least I had food now, and knew that I was not going to die on the road to Canaan.

« 3 »

The House of Ethbaal

THE CARAVAN FOLLOWED the great King's Highway into Canaan by way of Damascus, into a land of many hills and valleys and rocks, swift streams and awesome forests, and a great, snow-capped range of mountains towering over all. Many people seemed to live there, for the road was crowded at times, especially as we moved farther south. There were fields and villages and towns all along the way.

Having stopped for some light trading at the bustling town of Damascus, we turned westward toward the sea. The land was smoother there and it was not long before we passed the high, gleaming wall of Canaan's great city of Sidon; and, for the first time in my life, I smelled salt in the air and heard in the distance the sound of surf rolling in on the shore. And then, soon after, we came to Tyre.

The town of Tyre was on an island, approached by a narrow causeway from the beach. To come to the causeway, we had to pass through a tangle of miserable hovels of brick and mud, huddled about the shore. Never before, even in the worst villages at home, had I seen such dirt and smelled such smells; the huts were so crowded together that I wondered that the people who lived in them had room to breathe, much less move.

But then we came out upon the causeway and all the great sea was around us, and before us the golden, towered wall of the city with its well-guarded gate. Soldiers watched us as we passed through. They seemed to be of two different kinds, and one kind I had never seen before. They were slim, very dark, and clean shaven and wore nothing, it seemed, but brightly patterned kilts belted about their waists.

"What sort of man is that?" I asked the donkey boy.

"They are Egyptian soldiers from the garrison," said the boy indifferently. "They help our temple guards keep order and see that the city pays its taxes to Egypt."

I made a sign against evil. This was the first Egyptian soldier I had ever seen.

Never had I seen so many people crowded together as within the walls of Tyre. People thronged about the outdoor shops set up in the streets of the bakers, jewelers, vegetable sellers and the rest. Street musicians hung about, playing their instruments and looking for silver. Some of the streets were little more than alleys and it was hard to push your way through them. There were few horses and chariots about, but many donkeys and sedan chairs and simple carts.

In the middle of all this, we came upon an open place in which was a building surrounded by a courtyard.

"Is this the temple of Melkarth?" I asked the donkey boy; for Melkarth was the Baal, or patron god, of Tyre.

The donkey boy shook his head and, to my surprise, shuddered a little.

"No," he said. "This is the temple of Moloch." And he shuddered again, with a cringing reverence in the direction of the building. He said no more about it. A strange, cold feeling had come over me as I looked at it; and I did not know why, for the building itself was not ugly.

Hannibaal had told the donkey boy to guide me to his father's house. He had given me a letter for his father, written on a tablet of clay, to explain my arrival; for he himself had first to go to his father's warehouse. I looked with scorn at the marks on the tablet.

The house of Ethbaal was made of brick and wood and was three stories high, with a beautifully columned door. A servant took my letter, leaving me to stand in amazement in the entryway, gazing upon the splendor of bright tiles and ornaments and beautiful rugs, though the furnishings were few and simple. This was surely a great house of the city.

The servant returned with a message of welcome; and, as I was hot and dirty, I was shown to a room at the top of the house in which was a shallow tub and another servant to pour hot water upon me. This gave me great pleasure and the scrubbing I gave myself with soda powder set my blood to racing; so that when it was time for the evening meal, I found that I was ready to face these strangers unafraid.

Ethbaal himself met me when I came into the common room from washing myself. He was a small, elderly man, very thin and seeming never to be at rest. His hair was gray and he had a stringy beard, too thin to be held in a net as were the beards of many of the Canaanite men. But his eyes were sharp and kind, and he was resolved to make me welcome for his son's sake.

"The young Hittite," he said. "There are many of you about now, fine young men with fair skins and good, strong noses. You will make your way in Canaan, all of you. I must embrace you, for now you are as a son of the family."

And he did so, then led me to where the others waited.

"My mother," he said with great respect, "the lady Merris, whose youngest and only living son I am. She is the woman of the house, for my wives are dead."

I bowed to the lady Merris, who was very old and wrinkled and dressed with great richness, a mantle covering her white hair and heavy gold ornaments hiding her fingers and hanging from her ears. She leaned on the arm of a young girl who also wore gold rings and earrings and a golden headband. She was called Mehitabel and was the old lady's granddaughter, the youngest child of Ethbaal.

A young man stood behind her in the shadows, watching me angrily with large dark eyes. I thought at first that he was another of Ethbaal's sons; but Ethbaal called him his kinsman, and I saw that his eyes were just as angry when he looked at the others. He did not speak to me. His name was Jotham; and Ethbaal said that he came from the south of Canaan, somewhere near Jerusalem, the town of the Jebusites.

"My son is kept late at the warehouse," said Ethbaal. "But you are hungry, and we will not wait for him."

We seated ourselves on small Egyptian rugs about a low table and Ethbaal invoked the blessings of Adoni the lord, and El the almighty, all the Baals in general and Baal Melkarth patron of Tyre in particular, upon our meal.

It was a fine meal with roast pigeon, artichokes and strange, tempting cakes. There was wine too, though the mother of Ethbaal drank beer instead. Ethbaal explained to me that this was because she had come from Egypt, where beer was the favorite drink.

So the mother of Ethbaal too was an Egyptian. I looked at her with uneasy eyes. Ethbaal leaned toward me and spoke in a low voice.

"The family of my mother once lived in Akhetaton, the accursed city. Her father's father was brought up as a child near the court of the criminal Pharaoh, and her grandmother could remember his brother, the young Tutankhamen."

I did not know what he was talking about. I knew nothing of any Egyptians except that wicked Rameses who had fought us at Kadesh, and the very thought of that great and hated land was a dark and awesome mystery.

The mother of Ethbaal had raised her head and I could see how bright her eyes were among the dark wrinkles of her face.

"He was no criminal," she said in her old, whispering voice. "He was the true Pharaoh, the true and beautiful child of Adoni. There are no true Pharaohs on the throne of Egypt now."

There was an embarrassed silence. Then the young girl, called Mehitabel, spoke briskly.

"My grandmother is very old," she said, "and can say what she likes. *Her* grandmother told her many stories of the accursed city. It is so long ago that most people have forgotten it, and we need not be ashamed."

"It smelled of flowers," said the old woman stubbornly.

Now Ethbaal found his voice and changed the subject.

"Tell me of yourself, my son," he said to me. "Hannibaal says in his letter that your father was a man of property in Great Hatti. What did he raise on his land?"

"Wheat, barley," I said. "We had many orchards and kept bees. But mostly we raised horses on the grasslands." I swallowed hard, for my throat had tightened with longing for home.

Ethbaal was impressed. "Chariot horses?" he asked eagerly. "War horses?"

"The finest," I replied, remembering Labarnash.

"If that could be done here!" cried Ethbaal, raising his hands. "But this poor land is mostly for orchards and sheep. Still, we do a good business from the wool. Show him, Mehitabel."

The girl Mehitabel rose with pride and came for me to touch the cloth of her robe. It was finer and softer than any material I had felt before.

"From our workshops," said Ethbaal. "The finest. You see that it is bordered in the Canaanite purple. Only here can the purple dye be made."

"She jingles when she walks," said Jotham scornfully, and it was true, for there were silver ornaments at her wrists and ankles; but Mehitabel only smiled at him. It was the first time he had spoken. He seemed a strange young man, but everything in this house was strange to me.

I was pleased to hear Hannibaal's voice in the entry way, for he at least was not a stranger. I saw him through the door, giving his walking stick to a servant and having his hands and feet washed. He greeted me happily after having embraced Ethbaal and bowed to the grandmother, and I could not help being warmed by his sweet smile and gracious manner. Ethbaal was overjoyed to see him, and I could see that he was the pride of his heart.

"He is all that is left to me," he said. "There were four other sons, one who might almost have been a grandfather himself now, if he had married young. But he was the first born . . ."

Here he stopped and an uncomfortable silence fell upon us. I did not understand what the trouble was; but for some reason, I felt the same cold feeling that had come upon me once before that day, near the temple of Moloch. But Ethbaal did not say what had become of his first-born son.

"Two others were lost at sea," he continued, "and another of plague like my wives. Hannibaal is all that is left, but he will bring me honors I have no doubt."

He was silent for a moment. Then, as if shaking off some deep sadness, he turned to me, saying briskly, "And you, my son. What are your plans in Canaan? Are you a good man of business? Can you keep accounts?"

They were all smiling at me in encouragement, and I felt my face grow hot.

"I cannot read," I said at last.

There was a shocked silence, and I began to frown. Bookkeepers, traders, I thought angrily. Who but low-caste priests and servant scribes could read or write? High-born Hittites had better things to do than spend their lives over a thousand signs and pictures and learn to make marks in clay. But Hannibaal was smiling again.

"Here in Canaan," he said, "it is necessary for a man of position to read and write. It is not as it is in Great Hatti, where the sacred picture writing is a mystery in itself. Here we have an easy way, only twenty-two signs, from which all words may be formed. You will learn quickly."

"I do not care to learn," I said rudely. "I am not a scribe."

The young man Jotham snorted, but the others were patient with me still, explaining that in the coastal trading cities a man who could read and write and keep accounts could rise to great wealth and power.

"There is work you could do for me here in Tyre," said Ethbaal.

"But I am going to Harosheth," I answered.

"You cannot go there for a while," said Hannibaal. "There will be few caravans, for they say there is trouble again in the hills. You will have time to learn many things here."

And, his face alight, he talked for a long time of the wonders of the business and his father's possessions . . . farms where sheep were raised, workshops where cloths were woven, ships to carry the produce to the far corners of the world, and a copper smithy.

Ethbaal listened to all this, nodding his approval, and I wondered if Hannibaal would talk on through the night. At last, however, his father stopped him, saying that it was late and that prudent men did not waste oil for their lamps, and that it was time for prayers and offerings before bed.

And now a thing happened that surprised me more than anything I had yet seen. At mention of prayers, Jotham rose from his rug and walked from the room. The hair rose on the back of my neck; for, I thought, no man in his right mind would refuse to honor the gods. Though the gods had not protected me, I still feared them.

Ethbaal saw my look of horror and said to me, "Jotham must be forgiven. He has suffered greatly, and a man whose birthright has been stolen must always be bitter." And he added under his breath, "Those scoundrels down in Gaza!"

We said our prayers and made our offerings of incense before the household images and a little gold statue of Astarte the sacred mother. Then, as the lamps were burning low, we went to bed.

I found that I must share a room with Jotham. I decided that sooner or later I must speak to him. I did not know what to say; for, though he seemed to be a Canaanite lord, there was something different about him.

"Tyre is a fine city," I said at last, out of politeness.

"It is a den of evil," replied Jotham.

I decided to try again.

"The people," I said, "are very kind to strangers."

Jotham laughed. "Ask the strangers who make their purple dye how kind they are."

"But," I said, "how is it that you, who are one of them, should speak like that?"

To my amazement, he gave me such a savage look that I stepped back away from him.

"I am not one of them," he said.

After this he would not speak at all. And after a while he slept, leaving me to listen to the shouts of quarrelsome voices and the rattle of cartwheels outside, and to dream of the silent plains of Arzawa.

« 4 »

The Blue-Eyed Man

"WHO IS JOTHAM?" I said to Hannibaal. He was showing me about the city that morning, so that I could see the extent of his father's possessions and how he managed his affairs. We walked, for Hannibaal said that he could move faster than his chair carriers, who were very lazy.

"Jotham is our kinsman," said Hannibaal. "My father loves him, because his mother was his favorite niece and was lost to our family many years ago."

"But he says that he is not one of you."

"He is not," replied Hannibaal. "He comes of an evil and a blasphemous people. He is a Hebrew."

"What is a Hebrew?"

"They were men of Canaan, long ago. Then when the desert tribes and shepherd chiefs moved down into Egypt in a time of trouble, they were among them. They became conquerors and rulers there. The great dynasty of Egypt rose up against them and enslaved all those who were not driven out. Years later, some of their tribes escaped into the desert, returned to Canaan and took over many of the towns to the south from the Egyptian governors. They have been driven out of most of them and, with the help of Egypt, we keep them down as best we can. But they still make trouble for us."

"Then how is Jotham your kinsman?"

"His mother was my cousin. But she turned her back on her family to marry Jotham's father. Now, in the eyes of these Hebrew tribes, Jotham's father did wrong in taking a wife from the Canaanites, a strange woman as they would call her."

"Why is that?"

"Because they worship the desert God Jahveh, Who they now say is the same as El the almighty and Adoni the lord. They may worship no other but Him, for they say that He is jealous of the others. They call themselves Isra-El, the fighters of God. And our lady, the holy Astarte, they say is an abomination, and so are the Baals of our cities, and so are the beautiful images of our holy ones."

He was beginning to get angry, and I reminded him that he had been telling me about Jotham.

"Jotham's mother, our kinswoman, died when he was a child. His father, Amram, died a few years later. Amram was a prosperous man as these hill tribes count it. Jotham inherited flocks and herds; and all would have gone well with him, if he had not had an uncle in the south, in the town of Gaza, who is a real scoundrel."

I waited impatiently while he stopped to buy two cakes from a street vendor.

"Is this uncle a Hebrew?" I asked him, for I had assumed that they were all country tribesmen, living in the hills.

"Of course," said Hannibaal. "But he is a man of wealth and position in Gaza; and I have heard that he honors Astarte and the Baals like everyone else. He is a real scoundrel, though, and he wanted his brother's property too. So he went to Jotham's tribe and stirred them up against him. He said that Jotham had no right to his father's possessions in that his mother was a strange woman who had kept an image of Astarte in her tent. So they drove Jotham out, and the uncle got the flocks and the herds."

I felt a new sympathy for Jotham. But I wondered, since it was Tyre that had sheltered him when his own people had driven him out, why he had called Tyre a den of evil.

"Here is the street of the weavers," said Hannibaal, and I saw that we had come to one of his father's enterprises.

Hannibaal took me into one of his father's work-sheds, a dark place noisy with the rattle of shuttles. A man with a whip walked among the weavers, supervising their work. No voices were heard. The looms were worked by women and children. This surprised me, for at home slaves were seldom given regular work until they were grown.

I said so, and Hannibaal was shocked.

"We cannot afford such waste," he said. "Should we squander our longshoremen and our stronger women on light work such as this? Labor is expensive, and my father's workers are always well fed to keep up their strength. Where would my family be if we spent our money for no return?"

"They don't talk much," I observed.

"They are not allowed to talk. How much work would be done if the workers were allowed to gossip? Besides, we want no trouble among them."

"All the goods you make here in Tyre," I said. "It must take many slaves. How do you get them?"

"We trade for them among the foreigners," said Hannibaal. "And sometimes our merchants go to warring tribes or nations and buy up the prisoners of war at a low price. We can get them cheaply too from the slave traders of the desert. But it is cheapest of all to take them from among the Hebrews in the hills."

Hannibaal also showed me his father's copper smithy. It was a smaller shop than the weaving rooms and was hotter than I could bear because of the furnaces in which the metal was melted. The slave labor stayed by the furnaces, heating and pouring the metal. They seemed very pale. I suppose it was because they worked long hours, stopping only for a few minutes to eat, and for a few hours at night.

"Someday," said Hannibaal, "I will take you to the dye houses on the shore, where we send our cloth for coloring. Not till you become used to things though, or the smell will sicken you. The purple dye is made by grinding snails that have the coloring inside them. It is a costly process, for it takes so many of the sea creatures. Then too, the men who pull the grindstones must be the strongest slaves. That is why they are blinded, so there is no chance of their escaping. They are very expensive and, as the work is hard, they don't live long. That is why only great men can afford the purple."

I found that my morning meal was not resting so easily in my stomach.

Jotham was in Ethbaal's big warehouse on the waterfront and, when we reached it, he was counting bolts of cloth and making marks on a soft clay tablet with a reed pen.

Hannibaal gave him a pleasant greeting and asked if there was any work I could do, to show me how things were done.

"One who cannot read and write?" said Jotham sourly. "What work can *he* do?"

But he told me to climb the ladder and call off to him the articles that were stacked on the shelves so that he might list them.

"At least," he said, "you speak the language."

Before it came, I was longing for the midday meal. For, if the slaves of Canaan labored unceasingly, so did their masters. I was high on the ladder, shouting down to Jotham of three bolts of the thinnest wool, stained with the purple dye, when I heard a jingle as of little bells and looked down to see Mehitabel smiling up at me. She herself had brought the food . . . bread, cheese, wine and figs . . . and Jotham was angry.

"It is not right," he said, "for a woman of good family to walk in the streets alone."

"I did not walk," said Mehitabel. "I came in the chair and I covered my face. Come and walk on the waterfront while you finish your meal."

It was the hottest time of the day, but did not seem unpleasant with that strange, salt air blowing gently in from the sea. The waterfront and the wharves were made of stone whose heat burned pleasantly through my sandals. The wharves swarmed with longshoremen loading cargoes onto black, tub-like ships, urged on by foremen armed with bronze-tipped spears, who shouted commands in hoarse voices.

Down by a dock at the bend of the waterfront, cargo was being unloaded from a galley that had cast anchor. Mehitabel waved toward it proudly, saying that it was her father's, just back from a trip to the islands in the western sea.

"The ship master," she said, looking at Jotham, "will have presents for me."

"You do wrong to take his presents," said Jotham. "He is a treacherous man and your father is a fool to trust him." Mehitabel laughed.

A small boy was walking along the docks, accompanied by a manservant. He was dressed in a rich tunic of many colors and had sandals of the softest leather on his feet. The servant rebuked him for kicking pebbles with them. The people who saw him stopped and stared, and many kissed the sacred amulets that hung about their necks and made reverences. Mehitabel and Jotham stopped too, and when the child saw them, he ran to them. Mehitabel dropped to her knees beside him, kissing his hands and stroking his curly hair. He was a pretty child, but pale and cross looking, spoiled by all the homage he was receiving.

"Who is he?" I said when he had gone by, thinking him perhaps the son of the ruler of the city.

"He is a cousin of mine," said Mehitabel. "Jabin is his name. He is the first-born child of a kinsman of my father." To my surprise, I saw that she had turned pale.

Jotham had not bowed or spoken, but had stared at the child with eyes that seemed to burn with some strange feeling.

"Look away from him," he said. "He is already dead."

I turned to him curiously. A first-born child, Mehitabel had said. Ethbaal too had spoken of his first-born son and that he had died, but he had not said how. I opened my mouth to ask.

But before I could speak, a man nearby, carrying timber for a ship's hull, stumbled and fell, damaging the material that he carried. A spear-carrying foreman hurried over to him, struck him with the butt end of his spear and raised it for another blow.

Suddenly something happened in my mind, and I was no longer on the waterfront at Tyre. I was back in Arzawa and the captain of the sea people was beating my father to death. Without a sound I sprang upon the foreman, wrenched the spear away from him and struck him with it across the side of the head. I heard the people around me cry out. I felt a bleak joy and struck the foreman again across the jaw, knocking him down on the stones.

I might have killed him if another man had not come upon the scene at that moment, seized me and swung me aside in one powerful motion. And when I saw him I nearly did go mad. For he had blue eyes and curling bronze hair; so that when I looked into his face I thought I was looking at that same blue-eyed man who had killed my father.

I sprang at him too, but this time I was driven off in earnest. A big, powerful dog leaped upon my shoulders, snarling fiercely and bearing me down upon the pavement.

"Back, Pelops!" shouted the man, and the dog let go, still growling softly. The foreman, in the meantime, had recovered himself and was hurrying off, shouting that his master would bring charges against the family of Ethbaal.

I gathered myself together and got to my feet, staring at the stranger. He was, of course, not the man who had killed my father. He did not even look like him; for, though tall and strong, he was slender and graceful and elegant of manner. It was only his eyes and hair and height that had reminded me of the Achaeans at home.

He spoke to Jotham as if he knew him.

"Have you all gone mad?" he asked.

"Why did you stop him?" asked Jotham bitterly.

I stared at him in amazement and realized that his joy in the beating of the foreman had been the same as my own.

The stranger laughed suddenly and gave Jotham a scornful salaam.

"My apologies, young master," he said. "I forgot that the punishment of a servant might offend you. It is hard to remember that a lord of Tyre is a kinsman of slaves."

Jotham turned pale, but Mehitabel spoke hastily.

"Jotham is right," she said, surprisingly. "These men who wear out their labor in that way deserve to be beaten. Some of them even put children to work in the furnaces and mines and lose them before they are grown. Is it any wonder that they ruin themselves buying new workers? I have heard stories of you too, Achil, and how you drive your oarsmen."

Achil, it seemed, was the master of her father's ship. I guessed, from his looks and his manner of speech, that he was some kind of foreigner.

He was looking at me now, and it was with the look of the sea people in Arzawa.

"Who is this one?" he said. "Fair skinned for a Canaanite, isn't he? And such a fine nose. I can guess where he's from. There are many young ruffians of his kind nowadays, hiding about in safe corners of the world." He laughed and turned away.

I started toward him, forgetting the dog Pelops. But I felt a restraining hand on my shoulder and saw that it was Jotham's. We looked at each other curiously; and I knew that from now on we would probably be friends.

« 5 »

The Temple of Moloch

HANNIBAAL HAD COME to meet us, not knowing what had been going on. He and Jotham were to board his father's ship to check the cargo and the accounts, and he sent me on ahead with Achil to be shown whatever interested me.

I walked beside the ship master in sullen silence. He did not speak to me either, but swung along humming sea songs beneath his breath. Several times he slashed viciously with his staff at slaves and commoners who got in his way. I thought he did this out of cruelty rather than anger, for he seemed in a good enough humor.

The black ship was larger close to than it had seemed at a distance. Walking up the gang plank, I set foot for the first time on the deck of a ship and did not like it, thinking of the green water rolling beneath its hull.

Achil's cabin had fine hangings of goatskin, fine rugs and furnishings and, above all, ornaments and objects of art so perfectly and beautifully carved and molded and painted that I could hardly believe it.

Before I could ask him where they came from, voices were heard outside the cabin.

"Come in, come in, my young lords!" Achil cried as Hannibaal and Jotham followed us. "I have figures here and totals and the rattle of silver that will gladden your hearts. But first," and he bowed low to Hannibaal, "there are presents in my box for the lady Mehitabel . . . poor things, but they may give her pleasure. Let her come aboard when she wishes and take her pick."

Hannibaal nodded graciously, but Jotham reddened with anger. Achil saw it and smiled.

The business of the day began. Hannibaal and Jotham sat before a table, checking Achil's cargo list and weighing out the silver shekels he had received on his voyage.

I watched the proceedings of these merchants with scorn at first; then, to my shame, became interested. I would have liked to understand the marks on the tablets and papyrus.

The rest of the day we spent on the flat deck, watching and checking cargo that was taken from the ship . . . metals from the northern lands of Achaea, papyrus from the town of Byblos, other merchandise that Ethbaal would sell at a profit; and, of course slaves.

Some of these slaves were men who might have been of the people of Achil. But he showed no interest in any of them, except one. This was a well-dressed, assured young man to whom he spoke in a low voice before telling Hannibaal that he had bought him on his own and that he was destined as a present for the chief of Tyre. I thought that Hannibaal, for some reason, seemed disturbed at that. But he made no protest.

Hannibaal went home for the evening meal; but Jotham and I stayed late and food was cooked for us in the ship's galley. We ate on the deck and, toward the end of the meal, I saw gangs of men in chains being led up from below and walked about at the other end of the ship. Never had I seen men so pale and gray of skin, though some looked as though they might have been dark men naturally. The smell of them reached us and some of them, I could see, were so thin and weak that it was hard for them to stumble across the deck.

"Who are they?" I asked one of the sailors.

"The oarsmen," said the sailor. "Our captain doesn't believe in wasting much food on them when they won't live long anyway."

Jotham and I walked home together that night with a warehouse slave carrying a torch to light our way. We were silent at first, for I was thinking of all that I had seen that day . . . the wonder of the sea, the splendor of the ship master's cabin, the rich goods in the warehouse of Ethbaal; and also of the pallor and hopelessness on the faces of the children in the weaving rooms and the workmen by the copper furnaces, of what Hannibaal had told me of the dye houses, and the brutality of Achil.

Finally Jotham spoke.

"Do you still think Tyre is a fine town?" he asked.

"I don't know," I replied.

Suddenly he stopped still in the street.

"This is the heart of Tyre," he said. "Have you seen it?"

I looked about me and saw, with that strange cold feeling I had felt before, that we were in the open space in front of the temple of Moloch.

"Come on," said Jotham, and the torchlight made his eyes glitter. "Come inside."

I followed him into the courtyard with its trees sacred to Adoni, its pillar in honor of the serpent Shan and its image of the holy Astarte. There was an unpleasant odor about the place as there is about altars where animals are sacrificed. It was dark, but Jotham told the trembling servant to raise his torch; and the blaze suddenly outlined the figure of a great black image squatting within, its arms outstretched. I started and made the ancient sign against evil. Never had I seen so ugly a god.

"This is Moloch," said Jotham, "the lord of wrath, he who devours the first-born children of Canaan."

And all at once I understood.

"The oldest son of Ethbaal?" I said. "The little boy Jabin?"

"They are chosen from the greatest families of the cities," said Jotham, staring at the image, "and dedicated to Moloch in case a time of trouble should come upon the city. A fire is kindled in the lap of the god and the child is laid in his arms to die. All the city comes to see."

I began to shiver, staring at the black, outstretched arms, but I said nothing, for we Hittites had been taught to worship all the gods. After a moment Jotham shrugged and led me out of the place. We walked home in silence.

That night I could not sleep. I decided I never would till I had driven the image of Moloch from my mind; and, for a start, I asked Jotham some questions.

"Where does Achil come from?" I asked him.

"From the west. He is one of the sea people," said Jotham. And after a moment he added, "He is a spy. Did you see that slave he brought here for the chief of the city?"

"What about him?"

"He is no slave. But he will be in the household of the chief, and all that he learns there he will tell to Achil."

I thought of the ox carts and the chariots of the sea people at home and felt the old fear.

"Why," I asked, "should they send spies into Canaan?"

Then Jotham began to tell me about the sea people. And I listened eagerly; for I realized that, though they had destroyed my world and almost my life, I knew nothing about them.

"They are the children of Zeus the Thunderer," he said, "from the islands to the western mainland and up into the forests of the north, even beyond the river Danube. Some of them, like the ancestors of Achil, came down many years ago and married with the ancient peoples and became subjects of the old Minos of Crete."

"Minos?" I said. Here at least was something I had heard of. "The great kings who lived in the Labyrinth, the House of the Double Axe in Knossos, who bred the great bulls for the bull dances? But they were friends of our people."

"Yes," said Jotham. "All they wanted was our trade. But the earthquakes came and their great city of Knossos was ruined and the Minos was overthrown by his subjects on the mainland, the men with the northern blood in their veins. Now their great men are the sons and kinsmen of the Achaean Atreus . . . Agamemnon, Odysseus and the rest. They live in the old palaces and cling to what is left of the old arts and comforts. But new people are coming down into their land from the far north, more than ever before, and they say they need more room. So they are leaving their homes and coming into the east. They have come to Great Hatti. Next it will be Egypt, by way of Canaan. That is why they are sending spies into Tyre."

"But why do the Canaanites not stop them?"

Jotham shrugged. "The Canaanites are only slaves of Egypt. Why should they care if they change masters . . . if they can keep their riches and go on burning their children in the fire of Moloch?"

I lay for a while, turning all these new things over in my mind, then sat up on my elbow and stared at Jotham with curiosity and envy.

"How do you know all these things?" I asked him.

"I listen to the traders and sailors," said Jotham. "And I read what I can. It passes the time."

I was silent for a while. Then suddenly, to my own surprise, I heard myself asking, "What are those twenty-two signs that Hannibaal spoke of?"

"The aleph-beth signs?" Jotham sat up too and looked at me. "Do you want to learn?"

And so, till far into the night, we sat over a papyrus and did not sleep till I had memorized the twenty-two signs from which all the words of all the tongues of the nations might be formed. And I knew that in one night I had made myself master of what scholars before me, scholars of the ancient picture writing, had spent all their youth in learning.

But before I slept I asked Jotham one more question.

"To which of the sea peoples does Achil belong?"

"To a people from the island of Crete, Caphtor as we call it," he said. "The Egyptians call them Paleste. We call them Philistines."

« 6 »

The Princess and the Hittite Prince

I STAYED IN TYRE. I had not forgotten my promise to my father to go to Harosheth and find the man named Sisera. But, I told myself, I could go there at any time, and would be much better prepared by what I was learning in Tyre. Besides, as long as I intended to go, I had not really broken my promise. So I pushed it out of my mind, and soon it ceased to trouble me.

I learned quickly in the house of Ethbaal. Having mastered the aleph-beth signs, I soon learned to put them together into the words that appeared on the papyrus and tablets in the warehouse . . . words such as gold, silver, copper, bronze, wool, and shekels. I learned many other kinds of words too. There was a place in Tyre where books were collected, and sometimes I went there.

What I found in these tales and stories showed me a world that had gone on for thousands of years before the fathers of the Hittite lords had come down from the north and found it, and that had surely not always been the same.

I read stories of great nations that had risen and fallen and sometimes risen again under new names. Many of the stories were from Babylon. One that I read told of a great flood that had covered the world long ago. It told of a man who had been warned of the flood by the gods; so he had built an ark and saved himself and his family and two of every kind of animal, and become the father of all nations. There were books on sciences, too . . . the sciences of numbers and the stars who were, of course, the gods.

One night as I was walking past the hangings that separated the quarters of the lady Merris from the rest of the house, I heard music, voices and laughter coming from inside.

I was curious but did not dare enter without being invited. So I stood still and coughed as if I had taken the fever, till the hangings were pushed aside and the face of Mehitabel peered out.

"Come in, come in," she said. "You are just in time for the story of the princess and the Hittite prince."

I entered the apartment. The little Egyptian fox dog that belonged to Mehitabel barked angrily and nipped at my ankles, but I was used to that. The grandmother sat in a reclining chair, listening to the music of a flute played by a little servant girl in the corner of the room. And at her feet, to my surprise, sat Jotham.

The grandmother was telling stories of her youth in Egypt. They were stories she had heard from *her* grandmother, and I found out later that I could have heard them nowhere else but here. For these were the stories of the accursed city of Akhetaton on the Nile and of the accursed Pharaoh, with his one god. And these stories had long been forbidden by law.

The lady Merris did not think that the Pharaoh was accursed.

"His wife was the most beautiful of women," she was saying. "Nefertiti, the Beautiful Lady, they called her. He went nowhere without her and their six little girls and thought it no disgrace; and if the children laughed in the temple of the one god, she and Pharaoh would laugh too, even as they silenced them. And the temple was light and open to the sun."

"Who was the one god?" I asked her.

"Aton, the light of the sun they called him," she replied. "But he was Adoni the lord, and the Egyptians took him long ago from Canaan. Pharaoh said there was no other but him, that he was the lord of truth, and he moved his court from the city of the false gods and built the city of Akhetaton. No one may live there now. The priests destroyed him and his god and his city. The Beautiful Lady was banished from the courts and saw it all happen. But she lived to be old."

The lady Merris paused to preen herself a little, a look of pride on her face. “Once she visited the family of my grandmother. It was a great honor. She gave this to a woman of our family.” And she showed us the small image of a beautiful, delicate face. “This is the Beautiful Lady. It was made for her in her youth by an artist from Crete, who was one of the greatest of them all.”

I examined the beautiful face carefully, but Jotham looked only at Mehitabel. Mehitabel smiled at him, then spoke to her grandmother.

“Tell him the story of the princess and the Hittite prince,” she urged, and I looked up with a new interest.

“Ah, that is too sad,” said the grandmother. “Besides, it is the most forbidden of all.”

“But he is a Hittite and it will interest him,” said Mehitabel. “Besides, it is true.”

The grandmother smiled and shook her head, but did not protest again.

“It is the story of the second daughter of the Pharaoh of Akhetaton, for his oldest daughter and her husband were murdered by the priests even before his death.

“This second daughter, when Pharaoh died, was married to her father’s little brother, the young Tutankhamen, hardly more than a child; and the two of them became king and queen. But in his eighteenth year, the young king died.”

“How did he die?” I asked.

"It is said that Horemheb, the general of the armies, murdered him with poison. For Horemheb was a low-born man of great ambition, who wanted to become Pharaoh. To do this, it was necessary for him to marry the young queen; and the priests approved of this, for he was a faithful follower of the old gods of Egypt.

"But it is said that the young queen had once met a son of Subiluliuma the great, king of the Hittites, he who conquered all of Canaan, and had loved him. She knew too that he was strong and brave and would protect her against Horemheb and the false priests.

"So she wrote to the great Subiluliuma, saying 'Send me one of your sons, that he may be my husband and the ruler of all Egypt.' They say that the great Subiluliuma knew who it was she meant, and did send him to Egypt to be Pharaoh. And who knows? If that had happened, all the world might now be at peace and strong enough to drive out the people from the west."

"Why didn't it happen?" I asked her.

"Because Horemheb, that low-born general who wanted the throne for himself, heard what the princess had done and sent murderers to meet the Hittite prince on the road and slay him, which they did. But the princess died rather than ever be married to Horemheb."

"So Horemheb never became Pharaoh?" I asked hopefully.

"Oh, yes," said the grandmother. "For he became strong enough to take what he wanted even without marrying into the true dynasty. But the gods punished him for his wickedness."

"How?"

"He never had children. When he died his friend, the first Rameses, became king. His descendant is on the throne now. But they were never the true kings."

She lifted the little image of Nefertiti and gazed upon it.

"My grandmother used to pray that someday she would stand before the true king of Egypt and give this image into his hand. Once I prayed the same myself, but I know that it will never be."

Jotham, who had been listening closely, though he knew the story by heart, said suddenly to Mehitabel, "If I had been that Hittite prince and you the princess of Egypt, I would not have let them kill me, leaving them free to harm you."

"But if I had been the princess," said Mehitabel, "I would not have sent for you. I would have gone to you myself to keep you safe."

And I knew that Jotham and Mehitabel loved each other. I did not understand it, for he hated her golden hair nets and headbands and her hard heartedness toward the sufferings of the factory slaves. And she hated his scorn of the household images and the fact that he made her think about the factory slaves at all.

And so the days went by and I began to find some happiness in Tyre. I ceased to dream of the sea people in Arzawa. I even thought that perhaps I had found safety and would be able to live out my life in peace.

I did not know that a time was coming that would destroy all peace in Canaan. And I did not know that the day was coming closer when I would find myself a partner in the greatest crime known to the men of Tyre, a day that would change my life at least as much as it had been changed before.

« 7 »

The Sacrilege

THE SEASON OF the winter rains drew toward its close, and the time of the death and resurrection of the god Adoni was upon us, the festival of the first fruits.

The city was crowded, for many farmers and other people from out of town made it their business to come into Tyre at this time of year to take part in the religious rites.

We ourselves had gone to the temple, put ashes on our foreheads, bowed our heads to the dust in the courtyard, and bewailed the death of the god. The beautifully carved and columned door of the house of Ethbaal had been dutifully smeared with the blood of a lamb . . . one of the first-born of his own flocks in the country.

It was on the holiest night of all that the great sacrilege was committed. It was a strange night. There was something in the air that I did not understand. I had been busy in the warehouse for the past weeks, and had paid little attention to anything outside.

True, I had heard rumors and whispers here and there . . . three temple ships mysteriously lost with all their cargo . . . great fleets of warships massed on the shores of Crete and Achaea . . . a terrible insult from the Philistine ambassador to the chief of Sidon. . . .

It was, as I have said, a strange night. Outside, from time to time, we heard the clashing of cymbals and the shrieking of pipes and voices bewailing the dead god. And inside, the household of Ethbaal sat about their evening meal and did not even taste it. I could not understand this, for I was surely hungry.

I looked at them, wondering at their silence. Jotham was not there; but no one remarked upon his absence. And there was something in their faces that made me afraid.

"Achil the Philistine grows insolent," Hannibaal said that night to his father. Ethbaal did not reply to Hannibaal, and suddenly the young man sprang to his feet.

"Why should we listen to his insolence?" he cried. "He is our servant. If it were my place, I would have him beaten and forbid him ever to set foot on our ships again."

"Patience my son," said Ethbaal. "The priests are right. A time of trouble is at hand for the land of Canaan. But we have weathered such times before with our wits and our obedience to the gods. Above all, with our obedience to the gods."

Suddenly Mehitabel rose from her rug. Her face was a greenish white. She ran from the common room. Ethbaal looked after her nervously and I thought he half raised his hand as if he would make the sign against evil.

"What is wrong with her?" I asked.

"You must ask her," said Ethbaal. And he added strangely, "Remember that this is a holy night. And he who blasphemes in any way brings down the wrath of heaven upon his head and breaks the law of the land." He sat still on his rug, looking old and sick and sad. I still remember him like that; for, though I could not know it then, that was the last time I ever saw him.

I could not understand why he should have given me such a warning. I did not understand what it was that was hanging over the house. There was something in Hannibaal's face that made me shy of asking him, and Jotham was not there.

Later that evening I passed the fine hangings of the grandmother's apartments, heard voices within and asked if I might enter.

Mehitabel was seated by her grandmother, the little dog in her arms. It was trembling, having been made uneasy by all the noise outside. Mehitabel's eyes were red and swollen. The little servant girl was playing melodies on her flute in the corner, but no one listened to her.

"Something strange is happening in this house," I

said to them. "Achil the Philistine has spoken as if he were master instead of servant. And Hannibaal looks sick. And you turn pale at the mention of the gods and now I see that you have been crying. What is wrong?"

It was the grandmother who replied, her face hard as stone.

"She weeps for her cousin Jabin."

"Jabin?" I thought of the spoiled, sickly-looking little boy and frowned. "What is the matter with *him?*"

"He is to die tomorrow when the sun is high, in the fire of Moloch. And we, like the rest of the city, must see it done."

I felt as if someone had struck me a blow in the chest. Then, slowly, things became clear to me. The whispers and rumors about the insolence of the Philistines in Sidon. The three ships lost at sea. The boldness of Achil and the light in his eyes. All the activity that day near the temple of Moloch.

I understood. The shadow of the sea people had gathered over Tyre and all the coast of Canaan; and they were going to try to ward it off in the ancient manner, with the torture and death of a child.

"The priests have said that Moloch is angry," whispered Mehitabel. "They say he must have a gift to show our love and our fear of him."

The black image of Moloch rose before my eyes in all its ugliness, and I could no longer shut it out. Clumsily, I tried to comfort Mehitabel.

"It may be that something will happen before tomorrow," I said. "It may be that they will relent and save him."

Mehitabel looked at me with frightened eyes.

"Save him?" she cried. "And bring the wrath of Moloch down upon the city?"

I thought of the ox carts and chariots, the burnings and killings of the sea people at home and said no more.

"I will see it done," said Mehitabel. "All of us will see it. That is why we are favored in Canaan, that is why we have survived every trouble. Because we withhold nothing from the gods and we give our gifts gladly."

Suddenly she broke into sobs and hid her face in her arms.

"He is so little. He must be so frightened."

The grandmother took her in her arms, but her bitter eyes were upon the little image of the Beautiful Lady; and I remembered that only bread and wine were sacrificed to the one god of Akhetaton.

I could think of nothing to say. I wished that Jotham would come. Perhaps he could comfort her. I went through the house and into the courtyard, calling his name.

But Jotham was nowhere to be found.

All night the streets were noisy with passing bands of musicians, processions of priests, temple dancing girls, and celebrating people on holiday. Sometimes frenzied groups would go by the house, shrieking and slashing themselves with knives in their fervor.

Toward morning, however, much of the city became silent and deserted; for all the town had flocked toward the high place where stood the holy grove of Adoni the lord, where they would celebrate the rising of the sun and the resurrection of the god. Feeling the quiet outside, I rose from my bed and went out into the streets to walk.

But I found no peace. There were still the stones beneath my feet, and the high walls of brick and stone hemming me in, and the smells of the city were still there. And there was still the thought of what would happen tomorrow, in the temple of Moloch, when the sun was high.

Then suddenly it was no longer quiet. A group of armed guards from the temple garrison had come onto the water front. They asked me roughly what I was doing there.

"What's wrong?" I asked them.

"There has been a theft," said the captain shortly. "The warehouse of Ethbaal is to be searched. You had better come with us."

"The warehouse of Ethbaal? Searched?" I stared at them as if they had gone mad. Search the property of Ethbaal as if it were the hut of a slave?

"Ethbaal is an Elder," I reminded them. "Have you leave to enter his warehouse?"

"A great thing has been stolen," said the captain

grimly. "We have leave to enter anywhere, even into the house of the high priest, till it is found. Come with us."

The door of the warehouse yawned like the entrance to a dark cave and the temple guards were not anxious to enter, even with their swords and torches. They commanded me to go before them.

It was dark at first, and I stumbled about among the bales, wondering if there were anything in here and what it was we were looking for. A strange feeling had come over me, that something terrible and fearful was taking place; and not knowing what it was only made it worse.

After a while the warehouse became a little brighter from the torches but the corners were still dark. From the first, I had a feeling that something was there that should not have been.

Perhaps the guards felt the same thing and were uneasy, for they began to make an unnatural lot of noise, as if to reassure each other. They moved about aimlessly, thrusting swords into bales and barrels and shouting out threats to the unknown thief who might be hiding there. They seemed to have forgotten me.

Something caught my eye. It was a movement behind one of the bales in the darkest corner of all, and my skin began to crawl. There was too much activity among the soldiers for them to notice it and, drawn by curiosity in spite of fear, I moved toward what I had seen.

A dark figure stood behind the bale. A flare of

light crossed the corner and I saw who it was. It was Jotham and there was something with him, something small that was clinging to him and trying to hide. Then I knew what it was that had been stolen, and the hair rose on the back of my neck at the enormity of the sacrilege.

I moved back, then stopped, for I saw that Jotham was holding a knife. One of the guards was coming to the corner. I turned toward him, my body shielding Jotham and the child from his sight. I felt the point of the knife at the back of my neck.

"There is nothing here," I said.

The guard was a nervous young man who wanted to believe me. He hesitated for a moment and I felt my hands grow cold. One of the others called to him.

"Have you found anything?"

The young guard swallowed.

"Nothing," he said at last, and moved away. I started to follow, but felt an arm go tight around my neck, and again the point of the knife.

"Don't move," Jotham whispered. "Let them go. You stay here."

And, after stumbling about for a while longer, the guards gave up. Talking among themselves in troubled voices, they left the warehouse, and I was left alone with Jotham and the child.

« 8 »

The Boat

JOTHAM TOOK HIS arm from around my neck, but kept tight hold of his knife. He was trembling with fear and his eyes were bright and fierce.

"Do as I tell you," he said to me. "And you too," pushing with his foot at the frightened child. And to him he added, "Take off that robe."

"But it's cold still," whimpered the little boy, his voice shaking.

Jotham cuffed him and the child began to cry.

"Do as I say, or I will let them have you back. You," he said to me. "Bring me some of that dark stuff over there. Don't try to run or I will throw this knife, though you have been my friend."

I saw that it was wiser not to argue with him. Not wanting his knife in my throat I obeyed, stumbling about in the dark, for the sun had not yet begun to rise. I brought the bolt of woolen stuff to Jotham who, with his knife, slashed off enough to wrap the child and cover his purple-bordered tunic.

"Now go ahead of me," he said. "And if you cry,

Jabin, I will throw you into the water and drown you."

"Where will you go?" I asked him.

"To the mainland by boat," said Jotham. "You too."

With a sinking heart, for I was afraid of boats, I moved ahead of him to the door of the warehouse. There was no one about on the quay, so we went outside.

"Don't try to run," said Jotham again, flashing his knife in my eyes.

We made our way in silence down to Ethbaal's wharf, Jotham dragging Jabin roughly along behind him. There was a small boat there with oars and, at Jotham's command, the little Canaanite boy jumped in like a cat.

"Now you," Jotham said to me. I felt sick, looking at the frail thing swaying from side to side beneath me. But I closed my eyes, prayed softly to Teshub of the Double Axe, and jumped. My feet hit the shallow bottom of the boat and the world seemed to rock crazily about me. I almost went into the water, which would surely have been the end of me. But instead I fell to my knees and crouched in the bow, clinging to the sides and shaking with terror, while Jotham jumped and the rocking began again.

"Take an oar," he said, and, my knees still trembling, I started to obey him.

Then something happened. Another group of soldiers, Egyptians this time, had come onto the water front. Jotham was turned away from them and did not see them. They were coming toward Ethbaal's wharf and in another moment, if we stayed as we were, would be able to see us, for the sun was beginning to rise.

This was my chance. I did not even have to cry out and risk Jotham's knife. I had only to stay silent and I would be safe and the wrath of Moloch would be averted from the city.

I will never know why, but I heard myself saying softly, "Jotham, get down. There are soldiers on the quay."

Jotham fell flat on the bottom of the boat and pulled Jabin down with him, his hand over his mouth. I crouched too, as low as I could; and we lay still, the boat moving quietly with the water.

We listened to the sound of the men's feet as they came closer, and soon heard their voices above us. Jabin did not even whimper, and I tried not to breathe. Jotham's chest did not move, so I suppose that he too was holding his breath.

Finally they passed on. We lay silent till there was no sound but the lapping of the sea against the wharf. Then Jotham raised his head and let out his breath in a long sigh.

"It's all right," he said at last. "No one is here."

In silence we took our places in the boat. I had never held an oar before but found that it fitted easily enough in my hand. Before I realized what was happening we were clear of the wharf. Our progress was uneven at first, but I did as well as I could.

Jotham was looking at me curiously and I knew he was wondering why I had warned him. I was wondering myself. To steal the sacrifice of a god was an offense I had never even dreamed of committing or helping to commit, and I was sure that disaster would now follow me for the rest of my life. As for Jotham . . .

"Where will you go now?" I asked him. "You can never go back to Tyre."

"I know that," said Jotham. "When we are far enough south from the city, I will leave the boat and sink it. Then I will go inland, into the hills, where we will be as safe as anyone can be in this country."

"What's in the hills?" I asked him.

"Sheep and wolves," said Jotham. "Some towns and vineyards, rough land. Some things that are dangerous, like slave raiders and Canaanite troops. But you can dodge them if you try. Now what are you crying about?"

For the tears were running down Jabin's face and he was sniffing and coughing.

"I don't want to go into the hills," he sobbed. "I want my own house. I want my mother."

Jotham stared at him in disgust. "Look at him," he said. "Why is he worth it?" He stopped, looking pale and grim. I knew he was realizing, perhaps for the first time, just what he had done for the sake of this frightened, fretful little boy. For he was outside the law now, an outcast among the Canaanites as well as his own people. There would be no more books to read or peaceful rest in his great bed in the house of Ethbaal, and no more hours of happiness in the quiet apartment of the lady Merris. And he would never see Mehitabel again.

It occurred to me that I, too, might find myself under a cloud when I got back, and I looked at Jabin as grimly as Jotham did. But the child seemed to be tired from crying and sat pale and silent in the bottom of the boat. I took off my outer garment and wadded it into something like a pillow.

"Here," I said grudgingly, and shoved it in back of him. He laid his head on it and, after a while, slept.

"How did you do it?" I asked Jotham at last. "And how did you dare?"

"It was strange," said Jotham. "I never meant to do it. It just happened. I went out to walk in the streets and I saw a procession with this one," gesturing toward Jabin, "in the middle of it. The eunuch priests of Astarte were taking him to the temple to be prepared. But they were so taken up with wailing and beating their breasts for the death of Adoni that they were not even watching. He was so frightened he could hardly walk, and when he saw me, he called my name.

"I didn't even think. I just beckoned to him and he slipped away from them as easily as that. I had him down in the warehouse before they even knew he was gone."

The sun was high when Jotham finally pulled ashore. The heights of Tyre could still be seen, but we could surely not be seen from them. Jotham drew the boat up onto a stony beach, then shook Jabin by the shoulder.

"Wake up," he said, more kindly than he had spoken to him before. "We're here."

Jabin sat up, blinking fearfully. Jotham pulled him out of the boat. Then he looked at me.

"You will have to come with me," he said. "I must be sure of getting far away from Tyre before they know that I have left the city."

I shrugged. I did not blame him for not trusting me. It was always better, I supposed, not to take chances. I looked around me. The sun was shining and the air was fresh and clean. All was quiet and peaceful. I thought of the narrow alleys and high wall of Tyre, and the smell of the dye houses. I did not mind being Jotham's prisoner . . . for a little while.

But I was to be a prisoner for longer than I thought. And Jotham was not to be my captor.

« 9 »

The Hills

WITH SHARP STONES and heavy sticks, Jotham and I stove in the frail little boat. Then we shoved it out, filled it with stones and watched it go down. Jotham had brought along some cakes and from these we took a light breakfast.

"Shouldn't he have milk?" I asked, pointing at Jabin.

"Why?" asked Jotham, and I said I had heard that small children usually did, that sometimes they lived on milk. But Jotham said that I knew nothing about it and that Jabin would have to eat what we did. When we had finished eating, he said that the sooner we got away from the shore, the better.

We dared not follow the highway, but we knew that we wanted to go east; and both Jotham and I could tell directions well enough by sun and shadow and, at night, by the stars.

For a while the countryside was smooth enough, but later it became rougher and steeper. It was not long before Jabin began to stumble and Jotham, muttering to himself, had to carry him. After a while we took our turns with him. It was not the easiest way to travel.

Later in the day I heard a sound that made my heart quicken. It was the sound of a horse's hoofs and the rattle of chariot wheels. Jotham caught my arm and pulled me down behind a large rock.

"What is it?" I asked him.

"You will see," he replied, and I watched as well as I could from behind the rock.

A group of armed men came into view wearing the feathered helmets of the Canaanites. The leader rode in a chariot but the rest were on foot. Behind them walked or stumbled a line of tall, powerful men, barefooted or in rough boots, dressed in plain, straight, homespun tunics and with untrimmed beards. As they passed by, I saw that they were bound together with a heavy rope, passed from one to another about their necks.

"Who are they?" I asked softly, after they had gone by.

"Hill people," said Jotham. "Shepherds. Hebrews, probably of the tribe of Naphtali."

I stared after them in deep curiosity, remembering what Hannibaal had told me of these people.

"The soldiers have probably bought them from slave raiders," said Jotham. "The temples will either use them or sell them to private men. They all seem strong in that gang, so they are probably meant for the grindstones in the dye houses." He drew a deep breath and gazed hungrily about the soft, sunlit countryside. "They had better use their eyes while they still have them. All things will be dark for them soon."

He spoke calmly enough, but his face was pale.

"Why do they let them do it?" I asked.

"They have no leader, no judge," said Jotham. "We of the Hebrew tribes had great leaders once, but we have been scattered by Egypt and the Hittites. And the Canaanites, who bowed before their conquerors, are rewarded and can put their heels upon us."

"They should fight them," I grumbled to myself. "It is better to die fighting than to live as slaves." Then I stopped, ashamed, remembering how I had lived like a slave at home and had not died.

But now Jotham was warning me to keep my eyes sharp and my wits about me.

"There are things in the hills," he said, "that are worse than Canaanite troops. Men from the desert . . . Moabites, Midianites, Amalekites. They come in from the east through the valley of Bashan and lie in wait for travellers and shepherds. They have grown great and prosperous through their trade in men and women."

We had come upon a small stream at which we replenished our water skins and lay still awhile to rest. The soft smell of juniper and mulberry was in the air and Jabin, who had never been far from the city, lay sniffing the air and asking questions.

"There are lions out here in the country, aren't there?" he asked.

"Yes," said Jotham.

"Did you ever kill a lion?"

"No," said Jotham.

"I did," I told him, and gave him the story of the time a beast had come down upon our range and attacked some colts. I had not exactly killed it myself, but had held it off with a club and a knife till help had come. Jabin stared at me in awe; and Jotham looked at me with some envy and told Jabin not to talk so much.

We were not so easy in our minds as the little boy, for our food was nearly gone.

"We must get more," said Jotham.

"Yes," I agreed. "But how?"

"These lands are grazing lands," he said. "There must be sheep herders about, not far away. The tribesmen are hospitable and will take us in for the night at least."

He fell silent. He was looking no farther ahead than this one night, and I trembled, wondering what the days ahead could hold in store.

I looked uneasily about, and the country no longer seemed soft and sunlit. It was a rough, hard land here in the hills, with fearful dangers lying in wait, very different from the Canaan I had come to know in Tyre.

It was a lonely land too; and for the rest of the

day we saw no signs of human life and heard no voices but our own. It was not till the shadows had fallen that Jabin pulled at my robe and said, "There is a man over there, on that hill."

We looked and, through the dim light, made out a lonely figure on a ridge not far away. He carried a shepherd's staff, but had no sheep. Jotham hailed him.

"Stranger!" he shouted through his cupped hands. "Hi-yi-e-e-e!"

The man on the ridge heard him. He stood with one arm raised in greeting, waiting for us to come up to him; and he showed no fear, as I would have done if I had been alone in these hills, hailed by two strange men.

"Peace be with you," gasped Jotham when we had struggled up to his side. "Are you a Naphtalite?"

The stranger nodded, looking us over calmly. I saw there was no reason for him to be afraid of us, though we were two and he was only one. He was not tall, but was the most powerful-looking man I had ever seen.

"I am Jotham ben Amram," said Jotham, "of the tribe of Ephraim in the south. These are my friends. Are you from these parts?"

"From Kedesh, on the Jordan," said the stranger. He had a quiet, mild voice. His face was ugly; but his eyes made that unimportant, for they were deep-set and earnest and so wide open and direct that it was hard to look away from them. He did not tell us his name, but waited for Jotham to speak again.

"My friend and I have been travelling all day," said Jotham, and could not manage to keep his voice from quivering a little. "The child is tired. Do you know of people here who would take us in for the night?"

The stranger's eyes moved quickly over us, taking in our soft, finely woven clothing and our soft skins (for mine had softened too in the past year). Our earrings and ornaments were gone. We had sunk them with the boat, thinking they would only be a temptation to robbers; though we might have gotten a good price for them in some inland town.

When his eyes came to Jabin, clinging to Jotham's hand and staring at him hopefully, his face softened and he smiled a little.

"Follow me," he said.

We obeyed. I kept my eyes upon him, taking in his shepherd's robe, which was of good material and dyed in several different colors. He walked easily, like a man who was used to rough country and long journeys on his own feet.

By now we were again on smoother ground. Looking out across the valley, I could make out other figures, some flocks, and dogs who barked at the sight of us; and I knew that at last we had come to a dwelling place of the Hebrews.

A small boy saw our guide and ran toward him

with outstretched hands. A man followed more slowly. Both greeted him with such delight and respect that I knew him to be a man of renown in these parts. But they did not say his name, perhaps because we were there. Jabin, by this time, had fallen asleep in earnest and was bundled over Jotham's shoulder like a sack of grain.

These people, our guide told us, were of the family of Hushai ben Aaron, a rich shepherd of the tribe of Naphtali. It was two of Hushai's sons, a young man and a boy, who had come to greet our guide.

"Who are our guests?" asked the young man, whose name was Samuel. His words were polite enough, but there was no friendliness in his eyes. From the moment I saw him, I decided that I did not like him and that he felt the same about me.

"My friend is one of you," I said. "I am a Hittite, in exile from my country."

"And the child?" asked our guide. He was again looking at the fine cloth of the boy's tunic, with its purple border and dainty handwork.

"He is a Canaanite from Tyre," said Jotham.

"We will ask no more questions," said the stranger at last. "Later, when you have rested and eaten, you will tell us more of these strange things."

As they went before us, I heard him speak softly to Samuel and the boy.

"Do not say my name before these strangers, and tell the same to your father and the others."

On a level ground were the tents of Hushai ben Aaron. They were of black goat's hair and betokened the wealth of their owner, with rich curtains inside to divide one section from another. In the great tent of Hushai himself, to which we were taken, there was only one ornament. It was the small statue of a golden bull, which I supposed was a household image of their god. I was surprised to see Jotham look at it with scorn.

By the time we arrived, the women had prepared the evening meal, a kind of stew, well flavored with onion and garlic, and it was set out in a great, steaming dish.

We had awakened Jabin, and he was gazing about him with a look of doubt and fear. I could not blame him, for all was dim and close and strange to him. There were no brightly ornamented walls or tiled floors, no mother and maidservants to pet and scold him and wash his feet after his journey; and the firelight flickering from the torches cast shadows on the faces of those in the tent, making them seem rough and grim.

There were two women in the tent, Leah the head wife of Hushai and Tamar her daughter. They stayed in the shadows, not speaking and waiting to serve the men and see them fed before they ate themselves. The little boy we had seen before, whose name was Aphiah and who was the son of a second wife, was not so shy. He stood himself firmly before Jabin, gazing upon him boldly and reaching out to touch his fine clothes. Jabin shrank away, looking fearful and displeased. I was surprised that Jotham put his hand on his shoulder, as if to protect him, instead of slapping him for his cowardice.

There was little talk as we seated ourselves, cross-legged, around the common dish, except from Aphiah.

"That boy is from Tyre, father," he said. "Where the evil ones live."

Jabin did not seem to resent this, but looked at Aphiah with puzzled eyes.

The food was good, though more than once I burned my fingers, pulling chunks of meat from the steaming pot. After we had finished, a skin of cool water was passed around, from which Jabin drank thirstily, though he had eaten little of the food. At last the men settled back, satisfied. Hushai ben Aaron, the father, whose beard was gray but whose eyes were dark and bold, turned his shrewd gaze upon Jotham.

"Now we will talk," he said. "And you will tell us why you, you of the tribe of Ephraim, come to us from the city of evil, clothed in their finery and in company with a stranger from the nations?"

I began to be more and more uneasy. These people felt no friendliness toward us. Jotham had already been driven out from among them, and they hated my people. They were not like any people I had known before, and I wondered fearfully what we could expect from them.

"The tribe of Ephraim drove me out," said Jotham,

"because my mother was a woman of Tyre. But my heart is with the tribes and I wish to return if they will have me."

"And the child?"

"They would have made him pass through the fire of Moloch the destroyer. It was to have been today, when the sun was high. He is my kinsman and I have brought him away."

There was a murmur of astonishment at this, and Hushai turned his stern eyes toward Jabin.

"Come here, child," he said.

Jabin gave Jotham a frightened look. Jotham set him upon his feet and gave him a push toward Hushai, who took him by the shoulders and drew him closer.

"Weak and soft like all the Canaanites," he said harshly. "They have fattened him, haven't they, to make a fine feast for their evil god. Our God, who is greater than all others, does not ask the lives of our children, only of blasphemers and those who set themselves against Him. There are the seeds of evil in this child." And he looked so sternly at Jabin that the boy began to cry, though I could see he was trying not to.

The same anger seized upon Jotham and me, and we half rose from our places. But before we could speak, the young girl Tamar had come out of the shadows for the first time and had taken Jabin away.

"He is only a little boy," she said sharply, and I was surprised at how strong and bold her voice was.

"He is tired and has done no harm. He should be put to bed."

Hushai ben Aaron was suddenly no longer fierce and frightening. He looked guiltily at our strange guide, who was smiling a little.

"She is right," said the stranger. "Let her put the child to bed."

"No, no," cried Jabin. "I want to stay with Jotham and Uriah."

"Then you shall stay with them," said Tamar gently. "Where will our guests sleep?" She looked sternly at her father who shrugged, looked defeated, and turned the problem over to his wife. There was to be no more talk that night, for which I was glad though I was still not easy in my heart.

A place was made for Jotham, Jabin and myself in a corner of the men's quarters. The night air was cold and we wrapped ourselves well in our outer garments. It was hard to sleep for the smells of the cooking pot filled the tent, and the wind blew and there were strange noises outside.

"What is that?" cried Jabin at the sound of a long howl, close by the tent.

"Only a jackal," said Jotham. His voice sounded strange, as though he were listening in surprise to these sounds that he had not heard since childhood, and trying to remember how it had been before he had become a lord of Tyre.

"Do you think," whispered Jabin, "that Moloch will punish me for running away?"

"Moloch has no power here," said Jotham, in that same wondering voice.

This seemed to comfort the child, and soon he was asleep. But I lay awake till I heard the feet of Hushai ben Aaron and the stranger, returning to the main tent.

"This woman," Hushai was saying. "Will she come herself?"

"She will come," said the stranger, "and you will see. She has the powers of a thousand armed men."

What woman? I thought to myself. And why are they talking of armed men? But I was already half asleep.

"God be with you, Barak ben Abinoam," said Hushai, "and with her and with all of us."

So now I knew the stranger's name. Barak, I thought. That means Lightning. But he is not like lightning. And I went to sleep to dream of Barak riding in a chariot beside a mighty woman in gleaming armor, who had the strength of a thousand men.

« 10 »

The Knife Is Ready

THOUGH THE HANGINGS of the tent kept out most of the sun, there were streaks of light across the face of Jabin when I awoke. Jotham was already stirring, and I heard the sounds of women preparing food.

I thought that I would tell Jotham what I had heard before I had slept. Jotham listened and looked at me in amazement.

"Barak ben Abinoam!" he said. "I was told of him when I was a child. He is a great man of the Naphtalites, a judge of Kedesh and a great fighter. Once when he was young he led his tribe against the slave raiders of the Amalekites and there were no more raids for a year. What is he doing here?"

But I had other things to discuss with Jotham. For I had told myself that today would be the day when Jotham and I would part company. I had already half decided to go back to Tyre, explain what had happened and take my chances. Jotham was as safe by now as he ever would be, and I would surely say nothing to betray him.

But when I told Jotham this, he shook his head, and his words sent a chill into my heart.

"You cannot go back today," he said. "You cannot leave here, and neither can I."

"What are you saying?" I cried. "Who has told you this? Are we prisoners?"

"Hushai himself has told me," said Jotham patiently. "He has told me that there is trouble in the hills and that we must remain in his tents till it is proved whether we are friends or enemies."

I looked around in astonishment and anger at the big, bustling encampment of Hushai, noisy with the bawling of animals. Once again I met the eyes of Samuel. He was smiling now, and his smile worried me more than anything Jotham had said. Suddenly I found that I was afraid.

We went into the hills with the men that morning, as it was the custom among the tribes for guests to make themselves useful. We took Jabin with us, and he watched all that went on in wonder and growing delight. It was as new to me as it was to him, for my father had kept no sheep. I had always thought of them as placid creatures who would follow anyone or anything that led them, but it was not so. They ran and jumped and cried out and pushed one another till I wondered how anyone could have the patience to bother with the stupid creatures.

Jabin did not help matters. He was greatly excited

and ran about bleating like the lambs and laughing shrilly. Several times he sent them scattering and it was hard work to round them up again. Jotham, for some reason, had become very fond of Jabin and would not correct him; so it was I who finally shook him till his neck was nearly broken, and threatened him with worse if he did not listen and learn and stop running about.

Barak too had gone with us, and I watched in amazement his skill with the animals.

"Hi, hi, hi!" he would shout, like the loudest of the shepherds, using his stave like a marshal's staff, and it was hard to believe that this contented herdsman was a famous fighter and a judge of the town of Kedesh.

At midday we lay at our ease, ate bread and cheese and drank from a water skin, as we gazed far off to the north at the towering white tops of the great mountains, home of the gods.

"Baal Hermon lives there," said Jabin dreamily.

Samuel looked at him sternly, saying, "Baal Hermon has no power here. He can only stay on his mountain. He is not as the Lord, our God, Who can travel with us wherever we go, in the ark."

"What is the ark?"

It was Barak who replied, lying on his back, gazing intently into the cloudless sky.

"The ark is the golden house of the Lord, that our people built for Him when we found Him in the desert on the Sinai mountain. He is a God of fire and thunder; and our fathers say that when our people fled from Egypt they heard His voice and saw the light of His face on top of that mountain; and they knew that only He could keep them safe in the desert and bring them home again to Canaan. So they built Him the ark, that they might carry Him with them on the shoulders of four strong men, and have Him near wherever they wandered."

"Where is He now?" asked Jabin, sounding a little frightened.

Barak turned his head and smiled at him.

"In the south, guarded by the tribe of Ephraim, in a fine tent of many colors."

"Then how can He be here and protect me from Moloch?" Jabin sounded more frightened still.

"No other god can withstand Him, wherever He is," Barak assured him. But Jabin did not look too certain. Barak laughed and ruffled his hair. For some reason I found myself thinking of the lady Merris' story of the accursed Pharaoh and the Beautiful Lady, and how they had laughed with their children in the sunlit temple of their god.

But Barak did not smile or laugh with Jotham or with me; and the young man Samuel did not speak to us at all, only watched us now and then with that strange smile. Something surely was wrong. As the day wore on, my heart grew heavier and heavier with fear of what the night might bring.

Toward evening we kindled a fire for the evening meal. There was little talk, and I thought that Barak and Samuel seemed to be waiting for something. Even the little boy Aphiah seemed to know something that we did not and, when he thought we were not looking, watched us with scared, solemn eyes.

Nothing had happened by the time we had finished eating, and later we stretched ourselves in our robes by the fire and settled ourselves for sleep. I began to think I had been afraid only from cowardice and not for any real reason.

Jabin came close to Jotham and me, whispering, "Will it get too cold when the fire is out?"

"We must take our turns watching so the fire will not go out," said Jotham. "It will keep away the beasts, too."

"That's good," said Jabin and, almost before the words were out of his mouth, was asleep.

But I did not sleep for a while; and I knew that Jotham did not either, though he lay so still beside me. Once I looked at him out of the corner of my eyes and saw him, motionless on his back, staring into the dark sky. Nothing about him moved except his lips and I saw that he was whispering some soundless prayer. I shuddered, for there was no image before him. To what was he praying?

Deeply troubled I turned away from him and, after a while, slept. But my sleep was broken. I dreamt of my father, who gazed at me in my sleep with grieving eyes.

"Who are these people who despise our gods?" he asked me. "And what are you doing among them? Only evil can come of a broken promise."

Then his face dissolved into a blinding light and I awoke with a cry, the light of a torch blazing into my eyes.

Samuel stood smiling above me. "We have been called to the tents," he said. "The woman from Ramah is there."

I started to my feet and shook my head to clear it. I knew that whatever it was I had been afraid of was upon us.

"Woman? What woman?" I mumbled, remembering the talk I had heard between Barak and Hushai and my dream of the night before.

The firelight shone red on the dark young face of Samuel, making him look like some long ago savage out of the desert.

"She is a seeress," he said softly. "She has had many visions from the great God. She will tell us if your friend is a true man of Ephraim or if you are only Canaanite spies."

My heart sank, remembering the sacred Old Women of our villages at home, with their glaring eyes and their spells and curses.

"And," I said, "if she tells you we are spies?"

Samuel's eyes gleamed.

"An altar stone has been raised on a high place not far away," he said, his voice shaking a little. "The sacred knife is ready. If her judgment goes against you, the mighty Jahveh will have His sacrifice tonight."

« 11 »

The Woman from Ramah

CHANGES HAD BEEN made on the grounds where the tents were pitched. Two new ones had been thrown up, I supposed for the woman of Ramah and her servants, and they were finer than any I had seen before, striped in gay colors. The tents were all lit by torches and we could see that people were moving about within them in great excitement. Outside there was the tinkling of bells on pack animals and much braying of donkeys.

Leah, the first wife of Hushai, came to meet us, hastening toward her son.

"She is in the tent of your father," she said in a hurried, excited voice. "Your sister has brought water for you from the well. Hurry to make yourself clean. What a pity there is no time to dress the child in the fine clothes he wore last night. . . ."

"Mother!" cried Samuel.

"Oh, never mind," said Leah impatiently. "Go wash yourself."

Then her eyes fell upon Jotham and me and she fell silent and turned pale.

We went to the water buckets in the yard, which smelled of goats and sheep. It reminded me of the smell of the barnyards at home, so that my legs began to tremble a little less. It seemed we were expected to make ourselves very fine and, in sudden defiance, I splashed myself with water from the buckets and gave great attention to the braiding of my hair. I regretted that my golden ornaments and earrings had been sunk in the sea. If this were to be my death night, I wanted to meet it like a Hittite lord.

At last we were ready. Fear came upon me again as we walked to the tent of Hushai. At the entrance, an odor reached us that seemed familiar to me. I could just remember it from the old days at home, on the rare occasions when caravans would come to Arzawa carrying supplies from the far distant Hindus valley. It was the odor of a brew of tea leaves, which at home had been thought one of the rarest pleasures of the great world. To find it here in this wild place made everything seem stranger than ever.

We entered the tent, into the light of the torches. A little lady was seated on a pile of the best rugs and cushions owned by Hushai ben Aaron. Others had been set aside for Barak who sat beside her, watching her steadily.

This, then, was the woman from Ramah. She was far from being the wild-eyed holy woman I had expected. She was dressed in a fine woven robe of many colors, with a golden net upon her head. Her hands were little, delicate, and wrinkled and there were rings on her fingers. I supposed she was old, but her skin was fair and soft, her eyes bright and black. The family and servants of Hushai ben Aaron were staring at her as if she herself were a vision.

"She has a *house*," I heard Leah whisper to her son, "and lives all the year on her farmlands not far from the town of Gilgal, where the great altar stones are."

"Come into the light," said the woman, peering into the shadows where we stood. Her voice was not old at all, but brisk and strong. Hushai ben Aaron urged us forward. Jabin clung to both our hands, staring in awe at the sorceress; but he was not as frightened as he had been, for she was not nearly so different from old ladies he had known before.

She looked first at me. "A Hittite, of course," she said. "The fair skin, the braid, the manner of a lord and the hands of a farmer. Who could mistake him?"

I bowed to her with much respect; for she was surely a great lady, even though a seeress and a tribeswoman of the hill people, and even though she held my life in her hands.

"Come here, child," she said to Jabin; and he went to her trustingly, bowing with his hands to his heart like any well-bred little Canaanite boy. "Whoever they are, this one is harmless enough," she said. "Well, why are you staring? Have they told you I see visions?"

"Are you a seeress?" asked Jabin in a small voice. "Do the holy ones talk to you?"

"Sometimes the Holy One talks to me," said the woman seriously. "But not through magic signs and sacred dice. Tamar, put him to bed."

I saw that she wanted Tamar to leave as much as Jabin. The fear came back to me more strongly than ever, though I was glad to know for sure that Jabin was safe. Now the woman had turned toward Jotham, and her face had changed. It was hard and grave, like the face of a judge.

"You say you are an Ephraimite," she said to him. "From what part of the land?"

"My father had flocks," he said, "that grazed near Beth-El, the House of God, in the south."

"I know the people of Beth-El," said the woman. "I have not seen you among them."

"I have not been among them since I was a child," said Jotham. "But I have seen you."

"And who am I?"

"You are Deborah, the wife of Lapidoth," said Jotham. "When your husband lived, he sometimes let my father water his beasts on your land. You were the lady of the great house under the palm tree, the first of the tribe of Ephraim."

The woman Deborah beckoned him closer and looked intently into his face.

"I have seen a face like yours," she said. "And I have heard a story. Who was your father?"

"Amram," said Jotham. "Amram ben Omri."

The woman of Ramah sighed and closed her eyes. "Surely," she said, "that was the story."

Suddenly Samuel sprang to his feet.

"Any man can give a false name!" he cried. "And if he is who he says he is, still he comes from Tyre and has lived with the evil ones for many years. Condemn them both, great lady! A terrible time is coming upon us, and our God will be better pleased for a sacrifice!"

"Be still!" The voice of Barak was not loud, but it filled the tent. The torchlight shone in his eyes and blazed back from them, and he seemed like a man I had never seen before. Barak, I thought. Lightning. "Who are you to speak to a woman of God who has had visions? God will demand His sacrifice, not you or any of us here."

The eyes of the woman Deborah were fixed somberly on the image of the golden bull that Jotham had looked upon so scornfully the night before.

"*That* god would be better pleased for a sacrifice," she said, "whether of just or unjust men. He is not mine."

Samuel sat back angrily, muttering that the household image had been in his family for hundreds of years and had been brought with them from Egypt, but he said no more.

For a while the woman was silent, swaying slightly, her eyes closed. Suddenly they opened, she set her hands firmly on Jotham's shoulders and gazed deeply into his eyes. There was silence in the tent of Hushai, the family and the servants hardly daring to breathe. Her hands moved down his arms and fastened upon his wrists. I thought that she was seeing a vision.

"His eyes do not falter," she said, in a soft thin voice, "and his blood beats as calm as mine." Suddenly she pressed his hands and put him away from her. "God has judged. This is a true man of Israel. There will be no sacrifice tonight."

"If Deborah says it, then it is so," said Barak. There was a murmur of awe in the tent; and I felt myself beginning to tremble all over. I could not believe that it was finished, that I had really been saved from death.

Deborah turned again to Jotham and spoke in her usual brisk manner.

"I knew your father," she said. "And I knew your uncle better still. Those scoundrels down in Gaza." I had a shaky desire to laugh, she sounded so like Ethbaal. "But the tribes have seen the light and the curse of the judges has been upon your uncle for many years now. He does not dare return to the hills."

Suddenly Samuel, who had been very quiet, spoke again.

"What about him?" he said, looking at me. I saw that, as he was now forbidden to hate Jotham, he hated me more than ever.

Deborah looked at me for a long time without speaking. Though I knew I was in no more danger, I found that I could not meet her eyes. Even now I am filled with shame as I remember. For, though I did not know it then, I know now that my treachery to these people was already in my heart.

"There is no need for a judgment on him," said Deborah. "He is a stranger who has done us no harm. We have only to show him the hospitality that has been the custom of our fathers."

Suddenly, free of my fear of death, a great curiosity came upon me. Why was the woman Deborah here, why had she travelled so far? Why had a much revered woman of God come from the south to meet with a famous war leader and an important man of a northern tribe? Why were they so afraid of Canaanite spies and why had Samuel said that a terrible time was coming upon them? I was a stranger and I knew they did not trust me, but I promised myself that I would find out the answers.

I did not sleep that night and I heard Jotham, now moving restlessly beside me.

"Jotham," I whispered. "Are you thinking of Tyre?"

"Yes," said Jotham.

"If you could go back," I whispered, "would you?"

"I would never go back," he said quietly.

I saw that he meant it. The same look was in his eyes that had been there when he had lain so still, underneath the stars.

"She is a great lady," I said.

"Who?" muttered Jotham.

"The seeress from Ramah. She would have been a great lady, even in Hattusas."

Suddenly Jotham rose on his elbow, and there was a look of pride and joy and scorn in his eyes.

"Hattusas, that city of horse catchers? Does she not spring from a race of men who were lords in Egypt?"

« 12 »

"The Lord Is a Man of War . . ."

IN THE MORNING a fatted lamb was slain in the barnyard in honor of Barak of Kedesh and Deborah the wife of Lapidoth. All day the hired herdsmen tended the sheep alone while the family of Hushai prepared for the celebration to come. Fires were lit and the meat was prepared in great kettles, with the garlic, leeks and beans that accompanied it. Leah baked bread in an oven and Tamar made honey cakes on a pan over a fire of coals.

That night all the family of Hushai gathered in the main tent, together with the guests. The servants and herdsmen clustered about outside for their share in the feasting and entertainment.

There were two other guests that night, a man and his wife who had travelled in from the east and planned to pitch their tent in the plain not far from Kedesh. The man was a Kenite named Heber, not a

Hebrew; but his wife, whose name was Jael, was a woman of Israel.

Heber was a shifty-eyed, smiling man, who reminded me of the Babylonian traders of my childhood. He told everyone of his admiration for the Hebrews and his hatred for the Canaanites.

"My Jael can tell you what they are," he said. "She was stolen from her family by their troops when she was only a child. Out of pity I bought her from them and made her my wife."

But the woman Jael did not speak at all and only once looked at her husband, with such hatred that my blood turned cold. And when he spoke to her his voice was harsh and cruel. Looking at this silent, dark woman, I thought of my sister Annitis; and, for the first time, I was glad I knew for certain that she was dead.

Though Deborah was a woman, she was served first that night, for she was a holy woman. When family and guests had been satisfied, the rest was turned over to the servants. The meal was not silent tonight. Everyone seemed to have been seized with a strange excitement and joy.

Among the servants was one who could play the bagpipes and one who handled the drums with great skill. When the food was gone, the men began to dance the ancient dances, the dances they said were pleasing to their God, one by one, while the others clapped their hands, stamped their feet and uttered bloodcurdling cries.

"Do you know the dances?" I asked Jotham, clapping my hands with the rest, for none could resist the pipes and the drums and the stamping feet.

"I knew them once," he said and, for a moment, his eyes gleamed at the memory. Then his face saddened, and he drew back. "But it was a long time ago."

When they had tired themselves with dancing, Deborah offered us all a treat . . . a brew of the tea leaves of which she was so fond. Jotham's uncle, she said, had given her her first taste of the leaves as a gift, on one of his trading trips inland. But even this could not spoil her pleasure in them. She brewed the drink with her own hand, with much ceremony, then passed the pot around to each of us for a sip of the steaming, fragrant liquid.

While our hearts were warm from the pleasant drink, Barak asked her for some of the old songs and stories.

"She is a learned woman," he explained to us, "and knows all the histories of the tribes."

Deborah had with her a harp which she strummed softly as she began her stories. The light of the torches was on her face, making it seem somehow as ancient as the tales she told . . . stories of Abraham, the mighty chief from the outlands of Sumeria, who had been guided to Canaan by the great sky God El a thousand years before and whose people were the fathers of so many of the Canaanites and desert men; stories of the shepherd chief Jacob and his sons whose people had been lords in Egypt for two hundred years; of Joshua the mighty and Moses the law-giver, who had been a prince of Egypt.

"The Red Sea song," said little Aphiah, who was half asleep. "Sing the Red Sea song."

There was a sudden silence. Every voice and every movement ceased. I saw that what little Aphiah had said had some strange meaning among these people. I heard the wife of Heber the Kenite catch her breath and saw her eyes come to life for the first time. Heber himself was watching with an eager, puzzled look.

Deborah sat with lowered head for a moment, then seemed to make a choice.

"It is Barak," she said gently, "who must sing the Red Sea song."

And Barak rose to his feet and sang the song, while Deborah struck great chords on her harp.

"The Lord is a man of war;
The Lord is His name.
Pharaoh's chariots and his hosts hath He cast into the sea . . .
Who is like unto Thee, O Lord, among the gods?
Sing ye to the Lord, for He hath triumphed gloriously;
The horse and his rider hath He thrown into the sea."

Soft murmurs and even sobs rose among the people while the song was sung. Barak stood like a god himself, and it did not matter any more that he was not tall. And suddenly I knew what their secret must be. For this, I was sure, was a battle song, to be sung only in time of war. Jotham had said they had no leader. It seemed that they had found one.

« 13 »

The Raiders

THAT NIGHT, WHEN Jotham slept, I slid silently from my bed of robes. Deborah, Barak and Hushai, I knew, were not asleep. They had gone to Deborah's tent and there was a light within.

I snaked along the ground without a sound, as I had learned to do at home, and stretched myself along the tent pins, one ear to the ground and the other listening for every word from within the tent. Three dark shadows moved eerily on the colored hangings.

"There will be a council of the chiefs in Kedesh," said the quiet voice of Barak.

"So it has come at last," said Hushai softly.

"Yes," said the voice of Deborah. "Poor and scattered as we are, it has come at last. We have suffered slavery and death and the theft of our children. But when they command us to give our girls to the service of Astarte and build high places for Shan the Serpent, that is an insult to our God. That we cannot endure, even if we are utterly destroyed."

"We will not be destroyed," said Barak calmly. "We are not alone in this."

"The ox was sacrificed," said Deborah, "and its portions sent to the chiefs of all the tribes, in the old sign of war. But only you came to me, Barak. Only you were faithful."

"The tribesmen in the south," said Barak, "and in the cities on the coast, are men of property. They will not risk their wealth or their safety. But we are not alone. I have had word from runners. The chiefs of Issachar and Benjamin in the hills have heard us at last, and of Zebulon too. They will be in Kedesh within three days."

"Five tribes," said Hushai, and I could see his shadow counting on its fingers. "Will that not give us ten thousand men?"

My mouth fell open at this. Ten thousand men was a great army. It was surely some mighty host against which they planned to rise.

"And what of their chariots?" said Deborah. "And their horses from Egypt?"

" 'The horse and his rider,' " said Barak simply, " 'He hath thrown into the sea.' "

I could almost see Deborah smile. "Yes," she said, "and God has told me in a vision that they will be delivered into our hands. But He has not told me how."

"That," said Barak, "He has left to me."

"It will be as it was in the days of Joshua the great," whispered Hushai, "who leveled Jericho and drove out the Egyptian governors and raised the altar stones in Gilgal. The men of Israel will walk again in safety on the highways, and their stolen children will no longer die by the furnaces of Canaan, nor their strong men, grinding in the mills."

"We will raise our standard," said Barak, "on Mount Tabor, near the great salt lake. It will be a good place for men of the north and men of the south to gather. It will give us a stronghold and a place for retreat, where their chariots cannot follow. The hills have always sheltered us. They were why we were not utterly destroyed, even by the Egyptians."

"God be with us all," said Hushai again.

The talk was over, and two shadows lengthened as the men within the tent rose to their feet. In alarm I uncoiled myself and began my silent slide back through the undergrowth. My head was swimming with what I had heard.

But, as I moved, a shadow crossed me; and I could just make out in the darkness the figure of a man, dressed like a hired shepherd, hurrying away from the tent of Deborah. And so I knew that I was not the only one who had spied on that talk in the tent. But I could not see who it had been, nor could I speak of it to anyone without giving myself away.

Heber the Kenite, with his wife and servants, left the encampment early in the morning. They were to pitch their own tents in the valley, not far away. I stared after them as they left, wondering if one of them had been that shadow I had seen the night before.

When I had watched them out of sight I turned back to the tents, still thinking deeply, and into one of the most fearful and fateful days of my life.

First I quarreled with Jotham, so that he and I parted enemies that morning. This was the first bad omen. Next, I almost lost my life.

It happened because Tamar and I had gone to a spring for more water during the midday meal and had gotten out of sight of the others. I liked being with Tamar. She could do almost anything a man could do, but was gentle and kind as well. Besides, I liked to look at her. But this morning I was thinking of many things: of what I had heard outside the tent of Deborah; of the bitter things Jotham had said to me and of the things I had said to him; so I had little to say.

"Jotham is homesick," said Tamar suddenly, as if she had known what I was thinking. "That's what is wrong with him."

"Homesick?" I laughed. "He hated Tyre. He only wanted to return to the tribes."

"But the people of Tyre are his people too," said Tamar wisely. "In the ancient days before Abraham came, when the mother goddess ruled supreme in Canaan, they said that a child was more its mother's than its father's. Besides, he loves a woman of Tyre."

"How do you know that?" I asked, amazed. She only smiled. "If you're not careful," I said gloomily, "you will grow into another one such as Deborah. And she is a fine lady, but one such is enough."

Tamar was suddenly grave. "I will never be like her. She is a woman of God."

"Which one?" I asked angrily.

But Tamar did not answer. She was looking over my shoulder and suddenly I blinked in wonder, for I saw that her skin had turned the gray color of an olive tree.

I looked where she was looking. Four men, strangers, were standing together not far away and were looking us over, not menacingly but in a calm, businesslike way. Two of them had their heads together and seemed to be having a discussion.

"They have seen us," whispered Tamar.

"What is it?" I asked her. "Who are they?"

"Lookouts from a Midianite caravan," said Tamar in a dead, hopeless voice. "We heard they would pass here on their way to Harosheth. But I forgot."

For a moment the word "Harosheth" stuck in my mind. Then I forgot it, remembering what Jotham had said about Midianite and Moabite and Amalekite raiders. "They have grown great and prosperous by trading in men and women." For the first time I understood what it meant to be a Hebrew shepherd in the hills of Canaan.

"Tamar," I said, "run back to the others." Then I said, "No, not that. They will only follow and catch you; and if you lead them to the others, they may take everyone, for there will be more of them. Hide down behind that rock, and I will see what I can do."

Tamar obeyed me, though I knew she had no hope. The men were coming toward us. I stood back against the rock so that none of them could slip around behind me. I picked up a heavy, jagged stone and swung the sling that all shepherds carry to protect themselves and their sheep. The men came slowly, none of them wanting to be the one to get that stone. One of them moved out ahead of the others, and I fitted the stone into the sling.

"Be wise!" They called to me. "You Hebrews are outside the law. Raise your hand against us and you will be skinned alive in Harosheth!"

I swung the sling about my head and let the stone fly. It landed against the chest of the man in front, jerking him back, and he fell to the ground. The other three came together in a huddle. I picked up another stone.

"Rush him," said one of the men. "Kill him if you must. The girl alone should bring a good enough price."

I let fly another stone, which caught one of the men on the arm. He gave a great cry, but was not badly hurt. The three men came upon me in a rush.

I had time to pick up my stave and was able to catch one of the men across the jaw and send him sprawling before it was torn away from me. The other two got hold of me. I felt my arms and body twisted, something in my back forcing me to my knees, and cried out in pain and terror.

Suddenly I was jerked to one side, and then I felt myself free. The two men had forgotten Tamar. She had come out from behind the rock with a heavy stick and fallen upon the two of them. Never, since that day, have I thought that women are useless. Her face twisted and her eyes blazing, she brought the stick down upon the head of first one, then the other, and they fell at her feet.

But then it seemed as though she could not stop. She stood over one of them like the war goddess Anath and struck him again and again, crying bitterly all the while.

"Tamar, Tamar!" I protested. I climbed to my feet, got the club away from her and pulled her away. I made her run with me till we had gotten far enough from them to be safe; though, if they were alive, they were surely not able to pursue us. Then we sat down to rest, Tamar doubled over and sobbing as if she would be shaken to pieces.

"I hate them, I hate them, I hate them!" she gasped. "They took my sisters and three of my brothers and sold them to Canaan, so that only Samuel, Aphiah and I are left. If I could kill them and all the men in all the Canaanite cities, I would do it!"

"I know, I know," I soothed her. I even stroked her hair, which felt very pleasant. I had never known a girl like her before. I thought of her being dragged away to the copper furnaces or one of the dark, airless weaving rooms and shuddered. I thought of what I had heard the night before in the tent of Deborah, and for the first time my heart exulted as if I had been one of them. I even felt that someday I might come to understand Samuel.

The sun was low in the sky by the time we rose to go. As we started back to the tents, her hand was in mine. It was thin and strong, but small and soft and warm as well.

Jotham, I thought. I will find him and make it up with him. I know now why his heart is with these people and I will help him all I can.

But Jotham was nowhere to be seen, and it was Jabin who came to greet us.

"Uriah-Tarhund!" he shouted. "I have helped to kill a wolf." And he told how, while we had been gone, an animal had attacked some straying sheep, and he had given the alarm and helped drive it off. He was swelling with pride.

"Where is Jotham?" I asked him.

His face fell. "He is gone."

"Gone?" I cried. "Where?"

"To Kedesh. Barak and Hushai are going to do something very important there, and Barak chose him to go too." He brightened a little. "Samuel wanted to be chosen, but Barak said it was to be Jotham."

My heart was heavy with disappointment, but I was glad Jotham had been chosen. Tamar's hand was still in mine and I brightened too, thinking of the good day's work we two would have to tell about to the others.

Out of the shadows came Samuel and I opened my mouth to tell him the story of the day and receive his thanks for saving his sister.

"Let go of my sister's hand," said Samuel.

My mouth still open, I stared at him. With a shock, I saw that his eyes were full of wrath. All his anger at Jotham for being chosen had been turned against me.

"Go to mother," he said to Tamar.

For a moment Tamar paused. But she was too tired now to stand against anyone and, after a moment, she slipped away.

"Never speak to her again," said Samuel.

"I will speak to her whenever I like," I replied.

"Then I will kill you," said Samuel. "She is my true sister, the child of my mother, and I have the right."

He swung around and left me before I could speak again. I was filled with wrath. Even the water from the spring tasted bitter to me. Perhaps that was the real reason for what I did that night, even more than the memory of my father.

« 14 »

The Betrayal

SAMUEL AND I had been invited to eat in the tent of Deborah that night. Leah and Tamar were there too, but I neither looked at nor spoke to Tamar. I felt bitter even against her.

Deborah brewed her tea and passed it around in little bowls. She chatted with Leah like any other woman, of wonderful linens from Egypt, and camphors from the east for keeping moths out of wool, and the latest hair styles of the women of fashion in Babylon. After a little of this, I began to shift about rudely on my goatskin rug and finally yawned loudly in the middle of a remark about the new shops in the town of Shiloh.

There was an embarrassed silence. People were not supposed to yawn at Deborah. But Deborah was not angry.

"It is hard," she said, "for young men when the older men are away at council and there is nothing for them to listen to but the gossip of women. We will talk of other things."

And she began to tell us the story of a great battle of long ago in Egypt, when the finest army of Pharaoh had massed on the borders of the two lands to keep out a scattered and savage band of invaders.

"And which army do you think was destroyed?" she asked.

"I can tell you that," I replied, eager to show off what I had learned from books in Tyre. "It was the army of Pharaoh. For Egypt had no horses in those days and the invaders had gotten them from our people, the Hittites in the north."

And, I thought, if the finest army of Pharaoh could not stand against chariots, what could a half-armed mustering of Hebrew shepherds do against the chariots of Canaan?

Samuel was thinking the same thing, and he gave me an angry look.

"If the Lord had been on Egypt's side," he said, "she would have had no need of chariots."

"What would you have done?" said Deborah, looking straight at me.

"Why, why," I stammered. Then I collected my thoughts and spoke more surely. "If I had been the captain of Pharaoh's hosts I would have taken my men into the hills."

Samuel snorted. "Wise man! There are no hills in Egypt."

"There are hills here," I said, forgetting that I was not supposed to know what we were really talking about.

Samuel had forgotten too and, in his eagerness, he blurted out, "And do you think that Sisera is a fool who would risk his horses on rough ground?"

Sisera. The name, that I had forgotten for so long, hit me like a blow between the eyes. Sisera. "A man named Sisera. He will help you for my sake." I could feel the blood rush from my head, leaving me dizzy.

"Who . . . who . . ." I began, and then managed to finish, "Who is Sisera?"

Samuel now gave Deborah an uneasy look, realizing that he had said more than he meant. Deborah was silent a moment, then sighed.

"Our young friend is not a fool," she said. "I do not think we have hidden much from him. Sisera," she added quietly, "is the chief of Harosheth. He who is the captain of all the hosts of Canaan when they join together in battle. Have you never heard his name? They frighten children with him here in the hills. His hand is heavy as iron upon all of inland Canaan, and his evil city swallows its victims as a serpent swallows small animals, and even the Canaanites fear him. But he is a great warrior, who went to Carchemish in his youth and learned from the Hittites the arts of war and horses and chariot fighting."

It was the same man. My father too had been sent to the Hittite city of Carchemish in Amor, to learn of horses and chariots, for there were great teachers there. Once, when I was little, he had told me of a young Canaanite prince whom he had known there, whose life he had saved when a horse broke and ran with him, and with whom he had sworn friendship. But I had forgotten the story.

"What is the matter with you?" Samuel was saying.

For I was not able to sit still, but had gotten up and walked about the tent. I mumbled an excuse and sat down again, staring at the fire-lit faces.

Sisera was the chief of Harosheth. Sisera was the captain of the hosts of Canaan. Sisera was my father's sworn friend. These people were his enemies. And I sat among them and ate their bread. This was what had come of my breaking my promise to my father and blaspheming against Moloch. The gods had punished me indeed.

"Are you sick, child?" Deborah asked me. And she said it so like a mother that I wanted to cry; for I already knew the treachery that I was going to commit.

That night I told the others that it was lack of air within the tent that made me faint, and that I would sleep at the door of the tent. And, lying under the stars, I thought of what I must do.

I had taken the hospitality of the Hebrews and eaten food in their tents. To turn against them now would be a black betrayal. But to stay with them would be to break my promise to my dead father once and for all, and to set my hand against his friend; and that would be worse than any other treachery.

Besides, I told myself, these people were not my friends. Jotham was gone without a word. Tamar had not stood behind me. And Samuel. . . .

At the thought of Samuel, I knew what I had to do. I unwound myself from my robe and got up. The moon was still high. I crept to the tent door, listened and peered in to make sure that the others were asleep. Some moonlight from the entrance had fallen across the face of the sleeping Jabin. His mouth was a little open and his cheeks were flushed. Blasphemy or no blasphemy, I was glad I had helped to save him from Moloch. I wished that I could say goodbye to Jotham; and when I thought of Tamar, I almost wavered. But I did not.

There were skins in the yard and water in the well, and I supplied myself with what I would need to drink on a day's journey. I stole some cheese too from the tents, and some bread.

I had no time to lose; and, gathering up my supplies and setting my course by the stars I ran from the tents, heading toward Harosheth.

« 15 »

How I Came to Harosheth

THE NIGHT AIR was cold and I moved as fast as I could. I knew that Harosheth was somewhere to the southwest of Hushai ben Aaron's tents, but was not sure how far and did not dare to follow the highway. I seemed to be travelling a long way. The first light of morning was in the east when, to my great surprise, I heard my name called from a far off rise in the ground.

Three travellers were coming toward me. When I saw who they were I felt a chill, for they were Heber the Kenite and two of his shepherds.

There was a strange, sly smile on the face of Heber when he reached me; and his shepherds stood back, watching me with cold, curious eyes.

"You are far from the tents of Hushai," he said to me. "Surely my eyes do not deceive me, and your face is turned toward the city of Harosheth?"

I could not lie to him, and he smiled again.

"I too have business in Harosheth," he said. He grinned suddenly. "Better business than I had thought."

He said that he would guide me. I did not want to travel with him, for I did not trust him. But his two shepherds were very strong and I did not like the way they looked at me, so I did not want to insult him. One of them moved in an odd, furtive way. And suddenly I knew that he was the man I had seen in the dark, the night I had spied outside the tent of Deborah.

After we had walked a while I said, "Surely this is not the way to Harosheth."

"It is the way to the highway," said Heber the Kenite. "The highway will take us there."

"But is it not dangerous on the highways in these times?"

"Dangerous for whom?" grinned Heber. "I have no fear of the Canaanite soldiers, though they did me a bad turn when they sold me my wife."

I trusted him less than ever. Finally I stopped and said I would go no farther with him.

"Look behind you," said Heber.

I turned and saw the eyes of the two shepherds upon me with a look that made my blood run cold. I looked down from their eyes and saw that in their hands were their knives.

I said no more, for now I knew that I was the prisoner of Heber the Kenite. I began to walk again.

After a while, Heber went on talking.

"No," he said. "I have no fear of the Canaanites.

I have done them many a good turn and made many a good profit by it. No such good turn and no such good profit, though, as I will make today."

I said to him, "You will do them a good turn if you take me to Sisera in Harosheth. He will reward you."

Heber laughed. "You are right. My shepherds have had some talk with the servants of Hushai. They know that you ran away from Tyre of the Canaanites, and they know why. Yes, the men of Harosheth will reward me well for you."

"What are you going to do?" I asked him. But he did not reply, for we had come to the highway.

The highways were not as busy as they had been when I first journeyed along them from the north, and I knew it was because there were rumors of trouble in the land. But a number of men passed by, and even a caravan, and still we sat by the side of the road without moving. The hands of the shepherds were always on their knives.

"What are we waiting for?" I cried at last.

"You will see," said Heber patiently.

And at last I saw. A small squad of soldiers marched toward us from the south and, at the sight of them, Heber sprang to his feet. They were Canaanite soldiers, and they seemed to be guarding something of great value, carried among them in an ivory box.

Heber went to them, waving his hand for them to

stop. The captain gave the order for his men to halt, then listened while Heber spoke to him in a low voice. I saw him stare at me in astonishment, make the sign against evil, and start toward me. But Heber stepped in front of him, holding out his hand. They bargained together for a few minutes, then the captain gave him some silver and pushed past him toward where the shepherds were guarding me. Two of his men followed him.

Then something happened that I had never thought could happen to me. They pulled me to my feet and tied my hands behind me. They bound a rope around my neck, as I had seen one bound about the necks of the Naphtalites. My heart jumped and pounded, and my tongue seemed to freeze with terror.

"What are you doing?" I managed to cry out. "Why are you doing this to me?"

"This man has told us who you are," said the captain, pointing at Heber the Kenite. "The blasphemer who stole the sacrifice to Moloch in Tyre on the day of the first fruits. Even here in the hills we have heard of this. The city of Harosheth will have two prizes today. We carry the image of Dagon, lord of earth and sea, a gift from the king of Gaza, to guard our city in a time of trouble. Already Dagon has shown us his favor, for it is Harosheth who will avenge the insult to the lord of wrath."

I stared at Heber the Kenite, still not believing what he had done to me. Then someone jerked at the rope about my neck, I stumbled and choked, and we began our journey to Harosheth.

How I lived through the rest of that day I cannot remember, for when the rope did not choke me, the dust of the highway did, and, though the sun tortured me, they gave me no water.

I cannot remember my first sight of the dark walls of the city, on a height above a river, surrounded by its huts and stone cottages. But it must have been an awesome sight; for Harosheth, though surely not so great a city as Sidon or even Tyre, was the chief town of inland Canaan. "It swallows its victims as a serpent swallows small animals," Deborah had said. And I was one of the victims.

But I remember being marched through the gate and seeing that the people were bigger and rougher than in Tyre, and some wore many more and bigger jewels and ornaments; but their clothes were fewer and coarser, and some wore next to nothing at all. There was only one long street and a market place, a threshing floor and many alleys. There were no great buildings as there were in Tyre, except for one which I took to be the great house of the king.

The people stared at us and shrank back out of our way, and some of them spat at me. For they could see I was not a slave but a prisoner, a criminal of some kind. A beggar shouted something at me as we passed; and I think he put a curse on me, which frightened me more than ever.

"Father," I said to myself, "I promised to come to Harosheth. But not like this."

They took me to a prison, a dark underground place beneath the city wall. I was chained and given some water to drink, which I gulped down as though I had never had water before. Then they left me. I thought that I had been afraid many times before, but now I knew that I had never known what fear was. It was dark, and the air was wet and evil smelling, and I could hear the scratching and running of rats.

A guard brought me some food that night . . . at least I suppose it was night, for there was no light in any case.

"Listen," I said to him. "You must help me."

He did not answer.

"Can't you speak to me?" I asked him, but he only shoved the bowl of meal over toward me, along the floor.

"Listen," I said again. "Surely the lord of this city is a man called Sisera?" When he still did not answer, I said, "You must go to him. Or if you cannot go, you must have someone go for you. You must tell him that Uriah-Tarhund, son of Arnandash the Hittite is here."

The man turned to go, and I shouted after him, "Arnandash the Hittite! You must tell him that! He will reward you . . ."

But the man was gone. I had not seen his face, so

I could not tell if he had even listened to me. And if he had, would he bother to speak? And if he did, could I really be sure that this great lord Sisera was the man who was my father's friend, and what if he were not? I threw myself on the slimy wet floor and cried from fear, for I was still very young.

« 16 »

The Priest of Moloch

I CANNOT SAY how long they kept me in the prison, except that it was long enough for me to get used to the rats. They fed me enough and gave me enough water. But no one spoke to me. Sometimes, just for the sound of it, I talked aloud to myself and even laughed aloud at the clever things I said. Then, when I stopped, all would be more silent than ever, except for the dank drip of water down a rock somewhere. Then terror would come upon me and I would mumble frightened prayers to mighty Teshub, and even to Moloch.

At last, for the first time, the keeper spoke to me.

"Come," he said. That was all, and I followed him with shaking knees, my chains dragging behind me.

Some soldiers met us and took me from the keeper. They marched me through an underground way that twisted and turned and, finally, up some dark, narrow stone steps; then, so suddenly that I rubbed my eyes, into the light.

We were in a long chamber, smelling of cedar

wood from the northern forests. Through a window, I could see outside a high pillar in honor of Shan the sacred serpent; and nearby was a stone image of Astarte the mother, with a dove at her breast and the serpent himself at her feet.

I knew then where I was . . . in the chamber attached to the temple of the city god, where the town's council of elders held their meetings. There were benches at either side of the wall on which sat the elders in heavy robes of Babylonian style and with curling, heavy, netted beards. In the center was a higher bench. Two men sat upon it with another man, probably a temple scribe, squatting at their feet, holding a reed pen and papyrus.

I stared at the two men. I could guess who they were. One was thin and anxious looking with quick, bright eyes and a stringy beard, who reminded me a little of Ethbaal. I supposed that he was the chief elder.

The other man frightened me. He sat quietly on the high bench, unlike the elder who was always turning his head, gesturing here and there and whispering to the scribe. He had a heavy jaw and a thin mouth. His eyes were small and close set and, when he looked at me, it was like an icy wind going through me. He was clean shaven and dressed like a priest and I knew, with a sick feeling in my stomach, that he was the high priest of Moloch in Harosheth.

The guards stood me before the high bench, then

moved aside. The temple scribe began to read from his tablets.

"A great crime has been committed against our lord of wrath and, through him, against all the land of Canaan.

"This year in our sister city of Tyre, according to ancient custom, a sacrificial offering was dedicated to the lord Moloch of dreaded name, to appease his wrath. On the eve of the day of the first fruits, the offering was stolen, bringing down the wrath of the gods and all manner of evil upon all the land of Canaan.

"If this prisoner has conspired in this crime, he is worthy of the punishment for blasphemy, which is this: to be taken to the place of execution by the gates of the city and set upon with stones until he is dead.

"By our laws, two witnesses who will not deny each other must be brought forth. I ask leave of the lord elder to call them."

The elder gave his permission, and the first witness was called. He was one of the servants of Heber the Kenite. He is not a witness, I thought. He was never even in Tyre. He could not have seen what happened. But it did not seem to matter too much. An insect was buzzing about the chamber and I was watching it, shutting out of my mind what was going on around me, and taking a dreamy pleasure in the sunlight outside.

Then I heard my name. I jumped. It was the priest of Moloch who had spoken.

"What have you to say," he asked me, "of what these honest men have told us? Have they spoken the truth?"

"Part of it," I said at last, feeling too confused and tired to explain how much of it was true and how much was not.

"Then you admit your guilt, my son?" he asked, in a calm, kindly voice.

But I knew that he was determined that nothing should cheat his god and his city of their victim, and that there was no hope for me after all. The chief elder leaned toward him and began to whisper in his ear.

Perhaps it was because I realized that nothing could save me, or it may have been a fresh breeze that happened to blow through the window and pass across my face; but suddenly I was no longer drowsy, and my thoughts began to clear. I watched the two men closely and began to pay careful attention.

At last the chief elder turned back to me, smiling for the first time.

"My son," he said, "you must look upon us as your friends. It is painful to us to see one so young accused of such a crime, and to be forced to judge you so harshly. Remember that we are servants of gods whom you worshipped in your own country. It is your duty to put your trust in us as you would in your father, and tell us truthfully all we ask."

I looked at him and said nothing.

"Is it your desire," said the elder, "to redeem yourself in the eyes of Moloch, whom you have so gravely offended?"

"Yes, my lord," I replied. "It was never my wish to offend the gods."

"Then listen," said the elder. "We know that you took the sacred child to the Hebrews, and that you have been among them since then. We have heard rumors that the Hebrews are conspiring among themselves and are raising rebellion against us. Do you know of these things?"

"Yes, my lord."

"Then," said the elder, "give thanks to Moloch, for he has shown you the way to cleanse yourself of your great blasphemy. Think back to what you heard of these things in the tents of the Hebrews. Cleanse your heart of them and tell us what you know."

I stood staring at the two men on the high bench and thought of the dirty black image of Moloch as I had seen it in the temple at Tyre. I thought of the tents of the Hebrews, and Deborah, and Tamar's hand on Jabin's shoulder, and little Aphiah listening to the Red Sea song. A feeling that I could not understand came sweeping over me like wind across the grasslands at home and I wanted, for some reason, to laugh out loud.

"Answer the questions we will put to you now," said the high priest. His voice was harsh now, not soft and coaxing like the elder's. His eyes told me that redeeming myself in the eyes of Moloch did not mean saving myself from death under the stones. “Tell us their numbers,” he said. “Tell us their tribes. Tell us their plans.”

“No,” I said.

I said it as my father had said it before, to the captain of the sea people. There was silence for a moment. Then the high priest leaned toward me. His voice was soft and shaking with wrath.

“Then you are guilty of treason as well as blasphemy?”

“Treason to what?” I asked, looking at him scornfully. And, with all the pride I could muster I added, “I am a Hittite.”

When I said that there was a buzz of anger over the chamber, and an old hatred blazed into the eyes of all the councilors on their benches. I believe the elder would have liked to save me before, but not now. For there would always be hatred in the hearts of all ancient peoples for all their conquerors over the years.

The high priest of Moloch rose to his feet, his heavy face pale.

“You are insolent,” he cried, “besides being a traitor and a blasphemer. Do you know what happens to men who will not give honest answers? We test them. We test them in the ordeal by water.”

For a moment my head reeled. This ordeal was to be bound hand and foot, weighted down with stones and cast into the water. The priests had always assured us that those who spoke falsely or withheld information, would sink and perish; but those who spoke the truth would miraculously float. I feared the water above all things, far above even death by stoning.

"Will you give us honest answers to our questions?" asked the high priest.

"No," I said again, my voice shaking.

The high priest turned to the guards, probably to tell them to take me to the river. But I will never know for sure. There was a pounding on the heavy wooden door of the chamber and a voice called from outside.

"Open for the lord Sisera, Great One, captain of the hosts of Canaan, defender of the city of Harosheth."

« 17 »

The Ruler

THE DOOR WAS swung open. A man walked into the chamber and I knew that he, and no other, could only be the great one of the city and of all the hill cities of Canaan.

All the room seemed smaller for his entrance; for he was a big, black-bearded man, the tallest and broadest shouldered among them all. He had wide-set eyes, black as night under thick straight brows, and the nose of a hawk, a Hittite nose. Every curl in his rich beard was oiled, and it was held in place by a golden mesh studded with jewels. The rings on his hands, the gold collars and bands about his neck and arms, dazzled the eyes. The sacred medal about his neck was carved lapis lazuli, and a single emerald from Egypt, of great weight, studded his right ear.

All, except the high priest of Moloch, cringed and bent before him.

"The great chair!" called the chief elder. "Let the great chair be brought for the ruler of Harosheth."

"There is no time," said the lord Sisera. He sat

himself down unceremoniously on the high bench and the chief elder and the priest stood respectfully beside him. He sounded grim and angry. "Great things are happening. Even as you sit here I have had news that the town of Beth Shan has been raided by Hebrew tribesmen. Squads of soldiers have been attacked and slain by bands of shepherds. Never in a hundred years have they dared such things. It has begun."

A babble of voices began in the chamber, but was stilled when the ruler turned his blank dark gaze upon the elders. I stood bewildered in my chains, thinking that I had been forgotten by everyone. But all the while my eyes were on the Great One of Harosheth and my heart was saying, this man was my father's friend.

"The council will hear the words of the Great One without delay," said the chief elder shrilly. "Let the prisoner be taken back to the prison."

"Wait!" cried Sisera, and suddenly the black eyes were turned upon me. Their gaze struck me like a blow. "With what is the prisoner charged?"

"He is guilty, my lord," said the priest of Moloch, "of the highest sacrilege against the gods. He has cheated the lord of wrath in Tyre of his sacrifice."

The black eyes widened a little, but they did not seem shocked. I even thought there was a gleam of admiration in them.

"I do not know he is guilty," said the chief. "You, Uriah-Tarhund. Are you guilty?"

He knew my name. Perhaps the guard had gotten word to him after all. But I could not answer him; for by this time I was so confused and tired I did not know whether I was guilty or not.

"There is more," said the priest of Moloch. "The young man is a traitor to all the gods of Canaan." And, while my heart sank, he told the chief of Harosheth of their questions to me concerning the Hebrews, and of my terrible answer.

The Great One stared at me steadily for a moment. There was no expression in his eyes except for a kind of calculating look, and yet a cold sweat broke out on my forehead. Then he turned back to the elder and the priest.

"The blasphemy," he said, "was committed in our sister city of Tyre. Would you steal her revenge from our sister? Is this the time to turn the cities of the coast against us, when we of the hills have trouble in another quarter?"

The priest of Moloch leaned toward him to protest, but the Great One slapped his hand down upon his knee and spoke in a loud voice.

"Let the prisoner be taken to the Great House. All in Harosheth is mine. If he is the prisoner of Harosheth, he is my prisoner. I will judge him. And, if my judgment goes against him, I will send him back to Tyre. But. . . ." and he leaned toward the priest of Moloch and, to my amazement, winked suddenly. "But I will send him back in such a manner that when he reaches the gates of our sister city, he will not be alive to tell the tale. And so Harosheth will after all have the honor of his death, and yet Tyre cannot accuse us."

The chief elder nodded at this, looking pleased, but the priest of Moloch stood back, his eyes narrow and gleaming with anger. There was nothing, though, that he could say against the Great One. And so, more dazed than ever, I was taken from the temple. My chains were struck off, for Sisera had commanded it; and, under guard, they took me down the paved street of Harosheth, to the many colored Great House of the chief.

I had no time or heart then to look about me. I only remember that, once inside the Great House, I was taken in charge by a tall, powerful man and that when I looked at him I gasped; for he was as black as ebony, like the black soldiers from Cush who used to guard the Minos for pay in Crete, before the great earthquake. This one seemed to be a kind of servant, but there was a look of danger in his eye; and, when I was shut inside a room down a passage, I knew he guarded the door.

There was a great bed in the room, greater and more richly carved and inlaid than any bed in the house of Ethbaal. I laid myself down upon it and felt nothing but its softness, for I was too weary even to be afraid. Soon I slept.

When I woke it was dark and someone had lighted

the little oil lamp. Whoever it was had seated himself at the foot of the bed. I raised myself and looked into the shadows.

It was Sisera. In the dim light I could see that he no longer wore the splendid robe and ornaments of the Great One of Harosheth, but was dressed in a simple tunic and might have been any powerful, aging man, his black beard turning gray.

"You have slept well," he said to me. "No, stay where you are. You have a right to rest."

He rose and went over to the window, looking down upon the moonlit city.

"The wind from the hills is cool tonight," he said. "It is a blessing. Canaan is hot after the winter. Was it cold by the shepherd's fires?"

I swallowed a little, then nodded. "The nights were chilly," I said.

"And you slept in the open, wrapped in your robe and lived like a farmer. I know, I know."

Suddenly he turned toward me.

"I know who you are," he said. "When the slave from the prison spoke the name of your father it winded me for a moment; and, before I thought, I rewarded him, instead of having him slain for bribing his way in to see me. Your father," he added softly, then stopped.

When he spoke again, his eyes were glistening. "I have never seen Great Hatti," he said. "But it is half my home. My mother is a Hittite. Yes, she is the daughter of the Hittite governor who ruled in

Harosheth before the days of the battle of Kadesh. See, here is my grandfather's ring."

And he showed it to me on his strong, hairy-backed finger, a carnelian carved with the Hittite emblem of the double axe, just such a ring as my kinsman, the chief of Arzawa had worn. My chest swelled with tears I could not shed.

"Your father came to me in Carchemish," he said, "and saved me from a wild horse, like one of those Hittite heroes in my mother's stories. I loved him. I never forgot him. The stories he told me about that land that was half my home, how the wind blew over the grasslands, how all the men were strong and all the women beautiful, how the horses roamed the steppes. . . ."

Suddenly the tears I could not shed before overcame me and I found myself crying into my arms, while Sisera watched me with that strange, calculating look.

"Cry if you like, Uriah-Tarhund," he said. "There is no shame in shedding tears for a homeland you will never see again."

"Someday. . . ." I sobbed.

"No, you will never see the land of the Hittites again," said Sisera. "It is a land of strangers now. It is no more except in the hearts of its children and in its standard, which is here in the Great House of Harosheth. Would you turn against that standard, Uriah?"

"No!" I cried.

Suddenly Sisera bent over me and he was again the terrifying, god-like man he had been in the council chamber.

"Tell me what you know of the Hebrews," he said harshly.

And, looking into his cold black eyes, with the thought of the standard of Great Hatti in my heart, I told him.

"Five of their tribes have joined the rebellion," I said. "There is no danger from the coast tribes, for they will not join."

"How many will this give them?"

"Perhaps ten thousand men."

"Where will they meet?"

"On Mount Tabor, south of the great lake."

"Who leads them?"

"A man called Barak ben Abinoam, of the tribe of Naphtali near here."

Sisera heaved a great sigh, then sat down and wiped his forehead. I lay back on the bed, numb and exhausted. It is finished, I thought. I have betrayed them.

"All this is true," Sisera muttered at last.

"How do you know that, my lord?" I mumbled, not much caring whether he believed me or not.

"Because I know it already," he replied. "A man from the plain near Kedesh came and told me . . . for a good price."

"Heber the Kenite." I should have known before. "Then why," I cried, "did you make me tell?"

"Because," said Sisera, "if you had not told, I would have sent you back to Tyre, dragging over the ground at the end of a rope bound to a galloping horse. For, though I loved your father, I love Harosheth and the gods more; and those who fight for them I must know to be on their side."

I rose slowly in the great bed and drew my hand across my forehead in wonder.

"Then now," I said, "I am free?"

"I am your judge," said Sisera, "and I have found for you."

"But the priest of Moloch . . ."

"The priest of Moloch will bow before me like all the rest," said Sisera harshly. "I am Great One here. Now get up."

I obeyed him, as all must.

"I have something to show you," he said.

I followed him down the great stone stairway and into the dark street of the city. The black man, who I learned later was Sisera's armor bearer and charioteer and his bodyguard against assassins, walked silently along with us, as did a servant bearing a torch.

I drew the air of the fortress city deep into my chest. I should rejoice, I thought, that I am free again. But I could not rejoice. I could feel nothing at all.

As we walked, Sisera talked calmly of preparations for the fighting.

"There is little time," he said, "to send for horses and chariots from Egypt . . . if they would send them, and I think they would not. Egypt has troubles of her own in these days. But there are still horses in the north, chariots too, and our own workmen here in Canaan are becoming more skillful."

"How many will there be?" I asked him, not really caring.

"Enough," he replied. "Twenty horses for our troops are stabled here in Harosheth tonight. That is where I am taking you."

For the first time my heart stirred. There were few horses in Canaan except those imported for battle. These Canaanites do not love horses. I have seen them shiver at the thought of them, as I have sometimes shivered at the thought of an Egyptian cat. But already my hands were aching for the feel of the smooth skin over the moving muscles, for the touch of the soft muzzles in my palm.

They took me to the stables near the city wall, with its roofs of palm leaves. I could smell the well-remembered stable odor, hear the familiar stable sounds, the soft puffings and pawings. The servant held the torch aloft as I ranged over the open stalls, feasting my eyes on the handsome animals and whispering to them.

Suddenly I stopped. In one of the stalls was a stallion, a little larger than the others, of a shining honey gold. His ears were longer too, and his ribs strong as a barrel, and he had a look of horses from the south.

My heart beat faster.

"Where did he come from?" I asked. "He is not a northern horse, but neither is he a horse of the desert."

Sisera said nothing. I stepped closer. The animal whinnied in alarm, then bent his head and laid his muzzle against my neck. Then I knew.

"Labarnash," I said. "My colt. I raised him. I trained him. I gave him to the Great One in Hattusas because he was the best I had to give. Look how he knows me!"

My arms were around the strong neck, my face buried in the short, coarse mane. The Canaanite servant looked a little sick, but the startling eyes of the black man gleamed.

"Where did they find you, you beauty, you darling," I cried.

"He was the favorite of the young lord of Great Hatti, Subiluliuma," said Sisera, "he who would have been the second of that great name, had he not died with his father at the hands of the sea people. I found him by chance on a trip to Carchemish. He was in the stable of the young king's armor bearer, who had escaped from Hattusas after it was destroyed. He told me who it was who had given the animal to the king, and it seemed as if it was a sign to me, and I brought him here. If you had answered me falsely, he would have dragged you on your death journey to Tyre. But now he will draw your chariot in battle against the Hebrews."

« 18 »

The Hosts of Canaan

IN THE DAYS that followed, I saw little of Sisera. It was a time of quiet in Harosheth. The great men of the town conferred together and the people gathered about the walls of the Great House and the council chamber, hoping for scraps of news. Every day runners left the city with messages for other inland towns like Megiddo and Taanach. The air about the city was often alight and smoky with fire signals.

I was to serve in the hosts with the heavy chariots. But my training would not begin till we had marched out and the armies had gathered at their appointed meeting place. So for the next few days, I was much alone.

The mother of Sisera, with whom I would have liked to talk because she was a Hittite, was kept secluded with her maids behind her lattice windows, in the manner of Hittite women. The servants were not as they had been in the house of Ethbaal, where they would gossip as freely as the day was long.

Here they seemed sullen and afraid . . . and I understood why, on the morning that one of them was taken into the huge courtyard and beheaded in the sight of all the rest. He had, I learned, broken a vase of which the head wife of Sisera was fond.

So all I had to talk with was Memnet, the black man. He too seemed sad and sullen, but was not afraid. He had been sent as a boy, he told me, to Egypt from Cush, to serve in an Egyptian guard. He had been sent by the ruler of Cush. But the rulers of that once great land of the blacks had for many years been nothing but the slaves of Pharaoh, echoing his orders. Then his company had been sent to Canaan where Sisera had seen him and, impressed by his great strength and savage look, had made him his bodyguard.

"Would you like to go home?" I asked him.

"I would like to see the great city of Mem again, and the forests and the plains, and the prince in his ostrich-plume crown." He shrugged. "But it is not my home. For many hundred years my people have had no home."

I thought of my father saying, "It is not your home. It is their home now." To take my mind off that, I asked him, "How is it that you are not afraid of the Great One, like all the rest?"

Memnet threw back his head and laughed for the first time since I had known him.

"It is not all the rest who are afraid of the Great One. It is he who is afraid of them."

I did not understand this. I did not like to think of things that puzzled me, so I put what Memnet had said out of my mind.

"Labarnash," I whispered to my beautiful horse on my daily visit to his stall, "you and I will never understand this strange new world where everything changes from day to day, and nothing is what you think it is, and every minute you must make a choice. But you and I are together again, and that is enough."

The day came when we were to ride out to the encampment and meet with the hosts of the other towns. And for the first time I saw my chariot. It was not mine alone, for it was a heavy Hittite car for two riders and a driver. This was the great weapon of the Hittites, perfected by them and once used in the conquest of half the world, even to the borders of Egypt. It was sheathed and shafted with bronze and had swift round wheels, made more deadly by the sharp, costly iron scythes that stood out from them.

But suddenly, while I stood gloating upon it, I was shaken all over. Because, for one flashing moment I saw it as a terrible, murderous weapon for the crushing and tearing of Jotham.

The moment passed quickly, for Labarnash stood between the shafts. There were three horses and he, the strongest and the bravest, was leader. I mounted into my car and stood proudly beside the man who was my chariot mate. The Harosheth troops were all around me. They were a handsome sight, tough and bearded except for the young boys, dark brown from the sun and wind. We were all assembled by the gates of the Great House, waiting for Sisera to appear and take his place. He did not come for a while, and I knew where he was . . . in his mother's rooms, unable to tear himself away from her presence. For, of all people in the world, Sisera loved his Hittite mother best.

When he finally appeared, cheer after cheer went up; and I thought that, whatever the truth of Memnet's words, Sisera surely did not have to fear his soldiers. He mounted into his light chariot, shared only by Memnet, who stood straight and still as an ebony statue. For a moment nothing of either of them moved except Sisera's black eyes, which swept us all with their expressionless gaze. Then the Great One raised and lowered his arm in a swift gesture; the men began to march and the chariots to roll.

Many people were crowded into the main street of the city to watch us go out. Palm leaves were waved before us and heads were thrust through windows. We came to the city gates and I closed my eyes against the sight of the place of execution where, such a short time ago, I had expected to die beneath the crushing stones. Even now, executed men were hanging head downward from the walls. The sun streamed down upon me and Labarnash was in the traces before me. Still, I turned away my eyes.

The encampment of the hosts of Canaan was not far from the city. Its dark tents rose ominously, and all the ground within their circle was kept neat and unlittered as was pleasing to the gods. My chariot mate and I were to share a tent with two other young men. We were sent to our quarters and came face to face with them that first night. Both of them had been lying on their backs in silence; but they sat up when we came in, to satisfy their curiosity and welcome us after a fashion.

To my surprise, I saw that one of them was a Hittite, with his hair braided in the Hittite manner . . . from the north somewhere, I supposed, judging by his fair skin and light-colored eyes.

"Haruwandulis of Sinuwa," he introduced himself sourly. Sinuwa was on the Black Sea of the north, and the Sinuwans were a rough, suspicious lot who kept to themselves with their fish.

"This one," said Haruwandulis, pointing to the other young man, "calls himself Ahmoses. He is an Egyptian." He spat.

I stopped myself just in time from making a sign against evil. This was the first Egyptian soldier I had ever come upon at such close quarters, and I stared at him with great curiosity. He did not look evil, being very thin and rather frail looking. He had a dark face that I thought ugly, being thin and delicate but with a heavy, stubborn jaw.

There was something more about him, something strange. I kept thinking that I had seen his face before, though I knew it was not so.

"Do you play hounds and jackals?" he asked me.

I shook my head, still staring at him; and he sighed and lay back again on the ground. Later, though, he brought out his checkered board and offered to teach me the game.

But I refused. I had been told too many stories of Egyptian soldiers when I was a child, and I could not forget them. Besides, I noticed that he had brought with him no sacred medals or household images for prayer, as had all the rest of us. All he had was his hounds and jackals board and an old copy of the ancient Egyptian classic, Sinuhe the Stranger. I wished I could bring myself to ask to borrow it, for I had heard of it and often wanted to read it.

I mentioned this outside the tent to Haruwandulis.

"You let them make you read?" sneered the Hittite boy. "I took you for a soldier, a man of high caste."

My mouth fell open.

"As for *him* . . ." he jerked his thumb at Ahmoses and raised his voice so that he would hear. "I spit when I see him. Nothing but evil ever came out of Egypt."

He turned and strode away from me. I stared after him. His words sounded strange, ugly to my ears. And yet they were words I might have spoken myself a year ago. This was another puzzling thing that I put out of my mind.

In the days that followed, the hours of training were long and strict. Our hosts were made up of all kinds of men. There were Amorites and Aramaeans from the deserts to the northeast; Hittite mercenaries in exile from their country, like Haruwandulis and myself; Egyptians from the garrisons of Pharaoh in Canaan, some of them blacks from Cush like Memnet; and of course the Canaanite troops themselves, from Harosheth and Megiddo and Taanach, the great cities of midland Canaan.

And all eyes were turned toward the great tent of Sisera.

Sisera in those days had no desire to be alone. He would often invite one or another of his captains of a thousand to dine with him. We would hear with envy the sound of well-played music and loud laughter coming out of his many colored tent. I never dreamt of being allowed within those well-guarded precincts; so it was with great surprise that I looked up one night to see Memnet, stiff and magnificent, gleaming in his ornaments, standing before me.

"Uriah-Tarhund, son of Arnandash, you are summoned by the captain of the hosts," he told me. "You are to take wine with him tonight in his tent."

Haruwandulis gave me a look of stunned amazement. Ahmoses the Egyptian looked up from his book and said in a tomb-like voice, "Some people are highly favored in this world. Will you make me your armor bearer when you return, my lord captain of a thousand?"

"Read your book," I told him rudely. "It's all you

are fit for in the presence of a great man like myself."

He rolled it up and threw it at me, and nearly regretted it, for it just missed the common dish which had not been cleaned. We looked at each other and I found we were both grinning. It came to me with a shock that I liked him, Egyptian or not. But where was it I had seen him before?

Then I followed Memnet, and a feeling of excitement came over me at the thought of entering the great tent of the Captain of the Hosts.

It was more like a Great House than a tent. Woven of many colors, it covered much ground and was divided into large quarters, some of them for Sisera's servants and entertainers. Inside, it was furnished with costly rugs and the finest of carved and inlaid furniture. The image of Dagon that had been brought from Gaza was there for Sisera to offer to, of polished ebony with a head of lapis lazuli. And Sisera was there too, dressed as for a feast; but the tent was cleared of all except him and me and Memnet, who stood silently in a corner, and a girl musician who offered me wine in a cup of polished bronze.

"Drink, Uriah-Tarhund," said Sisera. There was a look in his eyes that I did not understand.

Wondering, I obeyed him, draining the cup to the last drop. The girl took it from my hands and slipped away.

"Now," said Sisera, and his voice was strange, "you and I together will pray to Teshub, king of Hittite gods, most mighty of all. For you are a true Hittite, the son of my beloved friend, and surely he will bless us both."

In the corner was the stone-cut image of Teshub as the bull; and it was to him we went, not to the gleaming image of Dagon. Meat burned on the little altar before him, and we bowed ourselves to the ground before it. Sisera pressed his ring with the double axe to his lips and we whispered the invocation, "Oh thunder god, oh my lord . . ." and nothing else was heard but the hissing of the meat on the little fire. And, though I did not know it, that was the last time I was ever to offer my heart to Teshub, god of the northern forests of my ancestors, god of the double axe.

When it was over I looked at Sisera with all my questions in my eyes and, as if I had spoken, he answered me.

"We move out in the morning," he said in his calm, flat voice. "Say nothing to anyone else. They will know when the sun comes up."

My heart beat faster. The day was at hand. Soon I would know what a battle was.

"One thing more," said Sisera. "If I should not come home to Harosheth . . . for who knows the will of the gods? . . . you must go to my mother. Remember, she is a Hittite woman."

He looked like a man who had seen an omen. And suddenly I knew what the look in his eyes was. It was a look of fear. But that could not be, I told myself. It would not be half-armed, wandering tribes from the hills of Canaan who would have the glory of the death of Sisera.

But Deborah and Barak and the Hebrew God came into my mind; and suddenly the thought came to me that even I might die. And what then? I did not like to think of the dark, sad underworld that the priests told of, Sheol as it was called by the Canaanites. The mother of Ethbaal said that in Egypt they taught that the very good would live with the gods themselves, but that the wicked would be condemned to a lake of eternal fire.

Well, I told myself, I had never done anything very wicked. Besides, after that one moment, I knew I was not going to die.

In the morning we were assembled into corps, with the squadrons of the chariots in the front ranks, flanked by the bowmen on foot. I whispered to Labarnash and talked to the charioteer of how to handle him.

"There is no holding him," I said, "but he understands the slightest touch of the reins. Remember, he belonged to the fourth Arnuwandas and the second Subiluliuma of Great Hatti."

The Captain of the Hosts had two dark horses from Egypt in the shafts of his light chariot. He was swathed in the Tyrian purple that I had always envied . . . till I had smelled the dye houses and heard of the blinded men who pulled the grindstones and did not last long at the work. The sun gleamed on his armor until, suddenly, a shadow came across it.

"It's raining," I said in surprise.

"It is too late for heavy rains," said our charioteer. "It won't last long."

My chariot mate had not yet arrived, and the charioteer told me he would not. At the last moment, he said, he had been transferred to another squadron and replaced by a new man.

"But why?" I said. "He and I have trained together."

My charioteer, who knew everything before anyone else, said that this new man had come late. He was from another city, he said, and had offered himself to the hosts of his own free will, as an atonement for some sin or other. Because he was a man of rank, he must serve with the chariots.

"It is too bad," said the charioteer, "but you are a skillful chariot man. So our captain of a hundred is putting this green one with you. Here he is now."

I turned and saw standing before me a graceful young man with a handsome, pale face, and a mouth that looked as though it had never smiled since the beginning of time. It took me a moment to realize that it was Hannibaal ben Ethbaal.

« 19 »

Wax and Mutton Fat

FOR THOUSANDS OF years, all the nations of the world had met in battle on the plain of Esdraelon. Men of the east, men from Sumeria and later Babylon, men from the desert, had battled there with the ancient inhabitants of Canaan, later settling down to mingle and become one people. Egyptians had come there and conquered the kings of Canaan on that plain. Joshua, the hero of all Hebrew stories, had fought there many years ago. Hittites had come down and conquered there, driving all before them, Egyptians and Canaanites alike. Now it was my turn.

We circled and entered from the south. We rode onto the level ground, divided by the great highway, with its fertile fields, its wheat and barley, its many flowers. All around us were the great hills. Always ahead of us in the distance was the mountain of Tabor, with its wooded slopes, rising from the plains like a great, lowering mound.

Often as we rode I stole a glance at Hannibaal,

but he never looked at or spoke to me. In that first moment, I had rejoiced to see him again. Then I had seen the change that had come over him. He had looked at me only once, then turned his head and kept silent.

By nightfall, we had reached our destination. We pitched our camp on the ground not far from Tabor. The rain still came down. But troops were put to work at once to dig trenches and barricades to guard the encampment from any surprise attack.

Ahmoses, Haruwandulis, Hannibaal and I huddled in our tent, warmed by coals of fire in a little pot. Sometimes we looked out across the valley toward the heights of Tabor, and thought we could make out dark figures among the flares that lit the lower slopes.

"Can you hear them sing?" asked Ahmoses. And over the wet night air came the faint sounds of shouts and chanting by many voices.

"They are dancing before their God," I said.

"We could show them some dancing of our own," said Haruwandulis, and broke into a battle song. But I did not join him.

"I could sing them a song," said Ahmoses; and I thought he would croon one of the sentimental songs of the Egyptian soldiers . . . "Seven days to yesterday" or "If you would come to me speedily . . ." But instead he bowed his head as if in prayer and sang softly:

"How manifold are thy works!
They are hidden from before us
Oh sole god
Like whom there is no other . . ."

"Shut your mouth!" shouted Hannibaal, speaking for the first time. The three of us stopped still and stared at him.

His face had gone white with fear and anger.

"Do you want to make sure that we all will die, with your wicked jokes? The song of the accursed pharaoh on a night like this! May the Baals forgive us all." And, with a little sob, he pressed to his lips the amulet that hung about his neck.

I looked at Haruwandulis and saw that he had turned pale.

The rain had lightened to a mist in the early morning, and word was spread that a champion was going out to challenge the Hebrews. This custom was strange to the Canaanites, though it was often done among the Hittites and the sea people. A champion fighting man would ride out in his light chariot and offer single combat to any champion of the enemy who would take up his challenge. Such a combat often decided the outcome of a battle.

We gathered with the others to watch, and I was not surprised to see that it was a Philistine who had ridden out. Several of the Philistine envoys to the inland towns had come with the hosts, more out of curiosity than for any other reason.

This man was splendid in his many-plumed helmet, decorated with the teeth of wild boars, with his white teeth and sea-gray eyes. He rode straight out across the plain, and I wondered why Sisera had sent him. Why should he take the risk of a single combat, when our chariots were strong enough to wipe out the enemy entirely?

"The rain is coming down again," muttered Hannibaal.

For a long time the Philistine rode back and forth before the lower slopes of Tabor, shouting his insults and his challenge. Then he rode back. We were close enough to see the anger in his eyes, and the dark frown on the face of Sisera.

"They are cowards!" cried Haruwandulis. "Barak, their great fighting man. Too much of a coward to take up a challenge, even when it was his only chance. Well," he turned to the rest of us, "why didn't they send out their witch Deborah?"

There was a shout of laughter. But Ahmoses, when we were back in our tent, looked at me with serious eyes.

"They say you know Barak," he said. "Why do you think he would let such a chance go by?"

"He is very clever," I said slowly.

"What is clever about it?" protested Haruwandulis. "It was his only chance against us."

"Sisera doesn't think so," I replied, remembering the black look on the face of the Captain of the Hosts. And a deep foreboding settled over me.

I was sleeping a troubled sleep that night, when a hand on my shoulder shook me awake. I forced open my eyes and looked into a shadowed face that was bending over me. It was Hannibaal.

I sat up with a violent start, my hand reaching for my knife. For so many things had happened to me that this was always my first thought.

But Hannibaal was not about to kill me. He sat back and watched me while I calmed myself, asking him angrily what he was trying to do to give me such a fright.

"I swore I would never speak to you again," he said at last, "or even say your name. But now I must, because I am afraid."

"Afraid of what?" I asked wonderingly; which was a foolish question, we being on the eve of battle. But somehow I did not think this was what Hannibaal feared.

"I have always been afraid," said Hannibaal.

I frowned in disbelief. Hannibaal the smiling? Hannibaal the lordly? Hannibaal, the master of such wealth and so many slaves? I felt as I had felt when Memnet said that it was Sisera who feared all the others.

"Always afraid," said Hannibaal. "Afraid of the Egyptian garrisons that they might take me away as a hostage, or take my father away if he could not raise enough tribute. Afraid of the Hittites, that they might come down and burn and pillage again. Afraid of the priests, that they might give me to the god if an unblemished first-born child of rank could not be found. Afraid of the gods. But most of all of Moloch. Always of Moloch." He wiped his forehead with a fine linen cloth, and I found that I was feeling a little sick.

"But," I asked him after a while, "what is it you are afraid of now? What is this sin they say you are atoning for?"

"Not *my* sin," said Hannibaal. "Yours and that other one's, who calls himself my kinsman. Seven other children were sacrificed in Jabin's place, to appease the god. The people spit on us in the streets . . . on *us,* of the house of Ethbaal. My father lies in his bed, and I think he is dying. And I must leave my home unprotected and offer myself in battle as an atonement for my family's crime against Moloch. *Now.* Now, when . . ." he stopped, and beat his clenched fist helplessly against his knee.

"Now, when what?" I prompted him impatiently.

"The sea people have begun their attack on Egypt. Our sailors have seen their fleets sailing south from Crete and eastward toward Sidon. The Egyptians make ready to withdraw their garrisons from Tyre and the other cities, to swell their troops at home. And my sister is there alone, my sister and my grandmother, with no one to defend them but a dying man and . . ."

"And Achil the Philistine," I finished for him, staring into the shadows in dismay. The night seemed to hang heavy like a blanket in the tent, and I had begun to tremble.

After a moment, Hannibaal said, "You must make me a promise. There is no one else. That is why I have broken my vow and spoken to you."

"What must I do?" I asked him.

"I will die in this battle," said Hannibaal. I caught my breath and made the sign against evil. "My family has offended Moloch, and I know now that only my death will appease him. You must promise me that, if you live, you will go back to Tyre and keep Mehitabel safe. There is no one else. You must promise."

I promised, for I had brought such trouble upon him that I could refuse him nothing. And for a long time after I lay turning his words over in my mind; while he, his mind at rest, slept peacefully beside me.

But I was to have no sleep that night. Not long after, Haruwandulis shook me by the shoulder.

"Are you awake?" he whispered.

"I am now," I grumbled.

"I have been awake a long time," he said solemnly. "Thinking. Uriah-Tarhund, was there an Old Woman in your village?"

"Of course," I snapped, and tried to bury my head beneath my robe. But Haruwandulis clung to my shoulder.

"Do you remember any of the things she used to do? Our Old Woman put a curse on a man they thought was helping Midas the Phrygian, and he sickened and died."

I sat up angrily. "What are you talking about?"

"What I have been thinking," said Haruwandulis, "is that if it would work for her, why would it not work for us?"

I stared at him, the skin beginning to crawl on the back of my neck.

"These things are very strange," said Haruwandulis. "All this rain when the season is past; and that Egyptian as good as *asking* the gods to turn against us. Your Hannibaal was right. Canaanites are not good for much, but they know about things like that. Look."

I looked at what he held in his hand and saw that somewhere he had gotten hold of a bit of wax and a piece of mutton fat. I began to tremble; for these things, in the hands of priests and Old Women, were very powerful.

"You are going to make a curse?" I whispered.

"Why not? Come on."

Feeling as if I were in a dream, I followed him to where the coals of fire were glowing balefully. Haruwandulis looked with some fear at what he held in his hand.

"Wait," I said. "It's blasphemy. Only the Old Women and the priests are allowed to make curses."

"But there is no Old Woman here," said Haruwandulis. "And Hannibaal was right when he said nothing could be worse blasphemy than that song

Ahmoses sang. Maybe this will help. At least we can try."

Solemnly he held his hands out over the fire.

"May our offering please you goddess, oh my lady of the lions, mother of the land of Hatti, queen of heaven and earth." Suddenly he cast what he held in his hands upon the coals and I started at the hissing, sizzling sound.

"As this wax has flattened, as this mutton fat has perished, so shall he who works evil against the gods of Hatti be flattened like wax and perish like mutton fat. So shall the tribes of Israel and their God be flattened like wax and perish like mutton fat."

The face of Haruwandulis looked red and strange in the light from the coals. The smell of the melting wax and sputtering fat made me sick. I could feel cold sweat on my forehead and on the palms of my hand. When the flame had died down, Haruwandulis sighed.

"Now they are accursed," he said. "I would have cursed Ahmoses too, but we need every man in battle."

He was smiling with relief and satisfaction and already looked half asleep again. He settled himself on the ground, wrapped himself in his robe and seemed ready to slumber till noon. Suddenly the feeling that had come upon me when I had said "no" to the priest of Moloch swept over me again. This time it came in the form of a great anger.

"Haruwandulis, you fool!" I cried.

He sat up and looked at me in hurt surprise. And then I uttered a terrible blasphemy.

"Wax and mutton fat!" I cried. "What kind of gods would have anything to do with that? What kind of gods would devour children and make war against each other? What kind of gods would keep men in fear from the day they were born? Shall I tell you what I believe? I don't believe there are any gods!"

I felt a great despair but, for the first time in my life, no fear of the wrath of the terrible ones. Outside I heard the sound of the rain, which had begun again in spite of Haruwandulis' curse.

« 20 »

The River Kishon

IN THE MORNING the rain had stopped. We went out onto the field where a high place and an altar stone had been raised. The priest from Megiddo, who had come with the army, was making sacrifice. An ox was being slain which raised our spirits, for the sacrificial meat would make fine food for the captains.

But we never ate it.

The horn of the lookout warned us first.

"They're coming out!" someone shouted. And then the sacrifice and the sacrificial meat were forgotten, though the priest and his attendants went calmly on with their work and their chanting, while horns sounded all around and captains of a thousand and captains of a hundred shouted their commands.

The tribes were coming out from Tabor. We could see them take form in the distance, a black horde moving over the ground in a swarm of uneven ranks. We could hear them sing, a blood-chilling chant from thousands of mouths. I could not hear the words, but knew what they must be:

"The Lord is a man of war!
The Lord is His name!"

Each of us knew his place. The horses were brought and charioteers worked swiftly to harness them, while the rest of us armed ourselves and fastened down our helmets.

"I wish there were a mirror," cried Ahmoses, "so I could see how I must look. Ah, Sinuhe the stranger! Like you I will strike terror into the hearts of the foreigners!"

My spear was in my hand and, at my side, the curved sword and battle hatchet, shaped in the holy sign of the double axe. Hannibaal and I mounted into our chariot behind Labarnash and the other two horses. Our squadron and the others formed into battle order beyond the trenches without commands from Sisera, so well were we trained.

Sisera drove his chariot back and forth along our lines, gulping down the remains of his breakfast and swallows of water to wet his throat, giving his orders to the captains of the squadrons, shouting so that as many as possible could hear his words.

"Let them come out well across the plains, too far to run back to their hills. Their numbers are greater than ours, as you can see, and they are counting on that . . . they have not even built barricades. But they are shepherds and the children of desert rats, and they will scatter before us like chaff before the wind! The scythes of our chariots will cut them down like wheat in the fields, and you foot soldiers will not even have to finish them off. They cannot retreat, for you can see that our chariots north of Tabor have already begun to roll! Remember your training! Remember the Baals! Wait for the signal!"

He rode back and a roar of cheering rose up from all our throats, then died down and all was quiet within the ranks. All of us strained forward awaiting the signal.

"It is time!" Hannibaal whispered to me. "It must be time!"

But still Sisera waited. And now the chanting of thousands of Hebrews was ringing in our ears. As they came closer they seemed to fill the plain, a great mass suddenly taking shape and color, so that we could see their rags and their nakedness, their black beards and the terrible anger that drove them forward. For a moment I felt a great fear.

Then, at a signal, the standards of the cities of Canaan were raised. The standard of Harosheth was the standard of the Hittites, and my fear was driven out.

The final signal came. The Captain of the Hosts lifted his spear and brought it down again. The horns sounded for the light chariots to ride out, and the air rang with their yells.

They rolled across the plain, into the ranks of the

Hebrews, cutting down all they met. But the Hebrews, though they were halted, did not scatter. Some of the drivers were pulled to the ground and some horses slain. But many more of the Hebrews fell. The cries were terrible to hear.

"You see," I said to Hannibaal. "That was old women's talk last night. You are not going to die today. It is they who are going to die."

A second squadron of light chariots was dispatched.

"Keep clear of the ruts!" shouted the captain. "Keep up your speed!"

By now all the ground between us and the enemy was being trampled and rolled into a mass of ridges and pools.

The shock of the second light cars had gained us a little ground, and there seemed to be some wavering in the ranks of the Hebrews. We knew it was time for the heavy chariots to move out and crush them entirely. The horns sounded for the leveling of our spears.

"Squadron ho-o-oh!" shouted our captain of a hundred. "For Astarte and the Baals!"

I felt the lurching of our chariot as it started forward; and in the same moment, I knew that something was wrong. We did not roll out across the field, gaining speed as we rushed toward the enemy. Instead we jerked and sank, started and stopped, went a little distance and finally came to a dead stop, our wheels mired down in the mud.

"What's wrong?" I shouted. "Start them up again!"

I looked around and saw that all across the field the heavy chariots were sinking into the ruts. Horses were straining, some struggling through, most brought to a halt as we had been. The rain had done its work.

The chanting of the Israelites had ceased. But now, among those who had not been slain by the light chariots, a terrible shouting and shrieking arose. Half ten thousand spear points were leveled at our breasts, and they came toward us at a dead run, swelling in size till they blotted out the sun.

"The whip! The whip!" shouted Hannibaal.

"No!" I cried. For the charioteer was beating Labarnash, and I could see that even his strength would not loosen the wheels from the mud. "Unharness him!" I cried. "He is useless to us now and they will kill him. Let him go!"

The charioteer did not obey me, and only beat the three horses more. In great anger, I jumped from the chariot and dragged him to the ground. I would have killed him, but all my thoughts were for Labarnash. I unharnessed him and struck him to drive him back, away from the spears of the enemy. He reared up above me, whinnying in fear.

"Go, Labarnash!" I cried. "They will kill you with their spears!"

But Labarnash would not go. He was afraid and puzzled and would not leave me.

The men of our hosts too were puzzled and afraid. Our unconquerable chariots were of no use to us now.

Some dismounted, to face the oncoming tribesmen on foot. Others stayed in their places while their drivers vainly tried to whip the horses forward.

But a few of them, Hittites or Egyptians, released their horses and mounted them, messenger style; and, together with infantry and dismounted chariot men, went forward through the mud to meet the Hebrews and break the shock of their attack. When I saw this, and seeing that Labarnash would not be saved, I sprang onto his back as I had so often done at home, and rode him forward into the ranks of the enemy.

"Go, Labarnash, go!" I shouted. And Labarnash obeyed me now, for he had been trained to attack. "Harosheth and Great Hatti!" I shrieked. "Hi-yi-e-e-e Teshub and the double axe!"

Haruwandulis and Ahmoses were among those who rode, each taking a horse from between the shafts of their chariot. We went swiftly. For these were good horses and, without the chariots, could cover wet ground as well as dry. We rode straight against them, foot soldiers following, coming into that milling mass of men with a shock that almost knocked us from our mounts.

Though the wheels and scythes were halted that would have torn and scattered the Hebrews, still for a while all went well. The tribesmen fought with clumsy spears and clubs and stones and ancient swords, while our arms and armor were the finest in the world. The warriors shied away from Labarnash and his trampling hoofs, I saw Haruwandulis clearing a circle around him with his axe, while Ahmoses was silent and skillful with his curved sword.

Many times I caught sight of Hannibaal, still in his mired chariot, raised above the field and fighting with the strength of seven Baals. Fear and hatred had transformed him. The glow of battle was on his face as I had never thought to see it, and he was as beautiful as Adoni as he killed many men who tried to drag him down.

Sisera too stood high in his chariot, a guard of men close about him. His bright helmet shone and his plumes waved as he tried, with shouts and signals, to bring some order into what was happening.

But order, now, was all on the side of the Hebrews. For, with our chariots gone, our training had failed us and each man now did as he pleased. The Hebrews, though, stood close. Captainless and ill-armed as they were, they had been well taught. Many of them had knowingly sacrificed their lives to stop the first shock of the light chariots . . . had, in fact, been trained and put in the front ranks for that purpose. Now they fought grimly and without disorder, heeding and following the signals of the ram's horn. And, little by little, we were beginning to give ground.

I saw them kill Haruwandulis. Still singing, he had ridden into a knot of the tribesmen and cut down some of them before a man seized him from behind and began to drag him from his horse.

"Haruwandulis!" I shouted. "Behind you, cut him down! I'm coming!"

I rode toward him, trampling all in my way, but it was too late. They cut him down with spears and swords; and, while I watched, someone seized the mane of Labarnash and, grasping me around the waist, dragged me to the ground. But the hoofs of Ahmoses' horse trampled him.

"Thanks!" I gasped and saw him laugh and raise his hand.

Now the tribesmen were thick among us, fighting like wild men. I had lost sight of Labarnash, though I thought I could hear his wild whinnying. I swung about me with my battle axe, trying to cut my way toward the sound.

I found him at last, and I saw him die. A fierce young fellow with a face like Samuel's and all his hatred for the oppressors and their horses in his eyes, had seized his mane and cut his throat.

I went blind then, and heard nothing but my own screaming and knew nothing but that I had killed the young man and was trying to kill him again and again. Then I made my way to Labarnash. I saw his eyes darken and his knees give way, while the blood gushed from his throat, and saw him sink to the ground in a great golden, broken heap. I fell across his body, and perhaps they thought I was dead, for no one touched me. While I lay there, I heard a voice shouting above the battle, a voice I remembered well, the voice of a shepherd, the voice of Barak.

When my head cleared, I rose to my feet and looked about me. Hannibaal no longer stood high above the field, but was lost to sight, and I knew that his words of the night before had come true. And then I saw that we of Canaan were no longer fighting for a glorious victory, but were fighting for our very lives.

They drove us back toward Megiddo, though some of us were already fleeing north toward Harosheth. All chariots had been abandoned, and even Sisera could no longer be seen. We no longer fought in squadrons and ranks, but every man for himself, and more and more among us began to break and run.

Through the day they drove us back, and pursued and killed us. And finally we gave up even the show of doing battle but fled before them, to our shame, and at last we came to the river Kishon.

This Kishon is not wide across. But that day it was swollen with the rains and, in some places, had overflowed its banks so that the ground was treacherous. The waters were yellow with mud torn from the banks, and leaped and churned as they pushed their way toward the sea.

I stood on the edge and could not take my eyes from those yellow waters. I hardly heard the cries and moans of our broken and fleeing hosts, filling the air around me. All I could hear was the rushing of the river.

"We have to cross," said a voice above me. I looked up and saw that it was Ahmoses, still mounted, and staring at the river with as grim a look as mine.

"I can't swim!" I cried, shaken with a cold chill.

"Then learn," said Ahmoses. "If you stay here, they will cut you to pieces."

"Then they will cut me to pieces. Better that than to be carried off by that water."

All around us men were wavering on the banks. Some began to enter the water. I watched one of them sinking deep into the treacherous mud. He struggled on, however, till he lost his footing in the middle of the river, and was swept away with pitiful cries that were finally choked off by the waters.

"I can't do it," I said again. For such a horror of the water had come over me that I was almost mad with fear.

Other men, too, had tried and met the same fate. And now some of them, in panic, had determined to stay and face the enemy on the water's edge, though they knew there were only two choices: to die on the swords of the tribesmen or to try to escape on the other side.

"Come," said Ahmoses. "My horse will carry me. Hang onto his tail. He will get us across."

"No," I answered, shivering helplessly.

"Then climb on behind me," said Ahmoses. "Maybe he can carry us both."

"I will not be the cause of your death," I said.

"Your horse can carry you to the other side. With me he will stumble, and you will surely drown."

The mouth of Ahmoses became thin, and his jaw looked more stubborn than ever.

"If you stay, I will stay," he said. "And then you will surely be the cause of my death."

I knew he meant it. So I mounted behind him, clinging tight around his waist and pressing my knees into the side of his horse. My eyes were tight shut, for I could not look upon the river.

I could feel the water surging up around us, as the horse's legs sank deep into the muddy bottom. But he struggled bravely and we were moving forward. Then I felt him stumble and almost lose his footing.

"Your axe!" I heard Ahmoses cry. "Get rid of your axe and your sword and your helmet!"

I obeyed him. The horse regained his footing, but only for a little while. Then he sank into the mud again and stumbled in earnest, throwing me sideways from his back. Without thinking, and to my shame, I clutched for Ahmoses to save myself. This unsteadied him, and he too slid from his mount and into the churning water.

I screamed when I felt the river closing over me, and then felt my scream choked off. But Ahmoses got hold of me around the neck. He was a strong swimmer, and sometimes he got my head above the water so that I could breathe. The river carried us far, but finally we both found our footing, even in the mud. Helped by some oleander bushes that overhung the opposite bank, we dragged ourselves ashore.

For a long time I lay gasping on the bank of the river, Ahmoses stretched out beside me. Anyone who had passed us might have thought that we were dead, but there were not many to pass. Those who did not try to cross the river were slain by the enemy, and many of those who did were swept away by the water; and those who say that all the army of Sisera was destroyed are very nearly right.

Through the night we lay on the river bank. All was quiet and the sun was rising when I finally brought myself to move. I was not wounded, except for a few cuts and bruises. But I ached all over from the flight and the battering in the river, and from weariness and hunger. Turning my head, I watched Ahmoses bow himself before the glow from the rising sun, in the manner of the Egyptians.

"Where are they?" I asked him, for all was so quiet. I struggled painfully to my knees.

"Don't stand yet," Ahmoses warned. "You nearly drowned and there is still much water in you." He crouched beside me. "They are dead as far as I know. And the tribesmen are following those who escaped, on toward Harosheth."

I sat back, trying to understand it.

"Dead," I said. "All of them. Hannibaal, Haruwandulis. I saw Haruwandulis die." I shuddered.

"I know. I saw it too," said Ahmoses. "But back

there . . ." he waved his hand toward the river, "one passed me who said he had seen that Sisera escaped north."

For a moment I was glad. Then I felt sick with shame at the thought of Sisera, coming down from his proud chariot and fleeing on his feet before the enemy. I lay back, staring at Ahmoses.

"The world has all gone wrong!" I cried suddenly. "You are an Egyptian and I am a Hittite, and yet you have fought beside me and saved my life. And we are beaten. How can it be?"

"Are you hungry?" asked Ahmoses. He was not wondering at all this. He was like a man whom nothing could surprise, to whom everything had already happened.

"I know I have seen you before," I said. "Where was it?"

Ahmoses shrugged. "We had better see about getting some food. But water, first."

We drank our fill from the river. It was not so rough as it had been before, but was muddy still and bitter.

"Have you a water skin with you?" said Ahmoses. "You had better fill it. To follow the course of the river will lead us toward Harosheth, and the Hebrews will be there. We must head west, toward the sea."

"What town is nearest?" I asked him.

"Megiddo, where my garrison was," said Ahmoses. "But the Hebrews will be there too. The nearest seaport is Dor. We had better go there. It should not be a day's walk."

"And then?"

"At least there will be someone there who will give us food."

We rose to our feet and I gazed back across the river upon the field of the dead.

"Labarnash is back there," I cried suddenly.

"Are you coming?" said Ahmoses.

"Haruwandulis should have a Hittite funeral," I said. "For thirteen days we should mourn him, with feasting. The fire that burns him should be quenched with ten jugs of beer and ten jugs of wine, and his bones laid in oil in a silver jar, wrapped in linen and a fine garment."

"Come," said Ahmoses. "How long can we live without food?"

But as we set out I wept for Labarnash, that he was dead and I must leave him alone.

« 21 »

A Promise To Be Kept

WE CAME TO DOR before the sun had set, and the walls of the town were bright with its last rays. There had been no fighting in this part of the country. There was the usual bustle and hurry about the city gate, with merchants up from the south and country people from nearby passing in and out, together with workmen and peasants from the miserable hovels outside the wall.

Many of them looked at us with suspicion, and many of them even made signs against evil or kissed their amulets when they saw us. But we could not be angry, for we knew how we looked. Ahmoses had washed off some of his dirt in the waters of the Kishon; but I had not been able to bring myself to do so, so great was my horror of it.

We were weak from the heat of the day, and with hunger.

A tall man in a sumptuous robe, with gold bands about his head and neck and gleaming curls framing his face, passed us by. A well-filled purse hung at his side. I stared at it with such hunger that Ahmoses put his hand on my arm.

"Be patient," he said. "With such a look in your eyes, we will never find a host."

"Peace be with you," said a man's voice behind us.

"And with you, gracious father," said Ahmoses, turning eagerly. "Are you a man of Dor?"

The man bowed his head. He was an elderly, kindly looking man, neatly but not richly dressed who glanced over our ragged garments and hungry faces with some concern.

"You have had a long day's journey I can see," he said. "Have you eaten?"

Ahmoses' fine manners deserted him and he answered simply, "No," with a quaver in his voice.

The elderly man smiled a little and said gently, "My home is yours, and my wife will be honored if you will eat her bread."

Ahmoses and I could have fallen on each other's necks for joy; but we restrained ourselves and thanked our benefactor with as much dignity as we could summon.

He led us down a narrow street, past a bakery and a jewelry shop, and past the public threshing floor, a bare flat stone where the farmers came to winnow wheat and barley. He brought us to his own house which was small, with only four rooms and a summer parlor on the roof, and with only one maidservant to wash the dust from our feet.

His wife brought the food to the roof of the

house and served us with her own hands. Never have I torn bread and onions so hastily with my teeth, or crammed into my mouth so many chunks of meat from the common dish, or drained with such relish a bowl of goat's milk.

The name of our host, we learned, was Elhanan. He was a scribe for the high priest of Dor, and sometimes made extra money by acting as a physician for the poor of the town.

Elhanan knew who we were and where we had come from. A caravan of merchants had brought word late in the day of a great battle on the plain, and already uneasy rumors were spreading about the town.

"Is it true that they were destroyed?" Elhanan asked me unbelievingly. "All the army of Sisera?"

"All destroyed," I answered. And I added wonderingly, for I too could not yet believe it, "We were beaten."

Elhanan asked us where our homes were, what our plans were and where we were going.

"There is work in Dor," he said, "if you want to stay. And my house is always open."

But I knew that I could not stay in Dor. I had made two promises, one to Sisera, one to Hannibaal. There were those who said that Sisera was alive; but Hannibaal I knew was dead. His was the promise I must keep, the promise to return to Tyre.

Ahmoses could not go back to his garrison at Megiddo. For by now Hebrew tribesmen were surely camped outside its walls, waiting for hunger to bring it to its knees; and its defenders had been slain in the battle.

"What will you do?" I asked him.

"I too will go to Tyre," he said at last. "Why not? It is a rich city and I had planned to go there some day in any case."

"How will you get there?" asked Elhanan.

I said I supposed we must walk as we had no money. Elhanan shook his head.

"Travel by land," he said, "will be more dangerous than ever in these days. To take the great highway alone is to ask to be killed."

"Surely," said Ahmoses, "there are still caravans that we could join."

But Elhanan held up his hand. He was thinking. "A ship," he said at last. "That would be the best way."

"But," I protested, "we have no money to pay for passage on a ship."

"In twenty days," said Elhanan, "a ship bound for Tyre will put into port here in Dor. I know the owner and the ship master in the way of business, and have done many favors for them with our high priest. It may be that they will be willing to do me a favor in return."

"Twenty days," I said, "is a long time to wait."

"It could be that you will be dead much longer," said Elhanan dryly, "if you take the highway."

So for twenty days we remained in Dor. To repay Elhanan for his hospitality, we tried to help him at his work, copying letters and accounts, going to some of the ships and taking inventory of their cargoes. Once at night I even went to a poor man's house beyond the city gate and held the basin while Elhanan pulled his tooth. I came closer to fainting than I ever had before.

What Elhanan did was no different from what Jotham and I had done for Ethbaal; but, not being a man of great family, Elhanan did not profit by it, or live in a great house. Yet I had never seen a kinder or a happier man. I never heard him speak harshly to his wife; and her greatest pleasure was to see to his comfort, weave the best cloth for his garments, and prepare him the finest meals at the lowest cost. He took her with him wherever he went, when not at work, not being happy without her company. And on the seventh day (which in Canaan as in Babylon is sacred to the gods) they would eat meals of bread and cheese and wine together on the roof, where Ahmoses and I joined them. Ahmoses told stories of Egypt and we laughed and talked as we had probably never done before in our lives.

But the day before the ship anchored which was to carry us to Tyre, the town of Dor was thrown into a state of terrible turmoil. An Egyptian ship, a "Byblos Travellor," put into port and its captain, without a word to anyone else, went straight to the headquarters of the Egyptian garrison. A little later, just catching the tide and without taking on or unloading any cargo, it set sail again.

The streets of the town began to buzz and churn with rumors. One sentence was repeated over and over again. "The Egyptians are moving out. The Egyptians are moving out."

Elhanan came home that night with a pale face and troubled eyes.

"It is true," he said. "The Egyptian garrison has been ordered home from Dor."

His wife dropped the earthenware dish she was holding, and it shattered on the floor. Nobody seemed to care.

"The sea people," said Elhanan.

I listened, unable to believe though I knew it was true, while he told how they had already begun to burn and raid in the north; how they had landed on the beach at Sidon and, when the great city resisted, put it to the torch; how Tyre had already hastened to throw her gates open to the invaders.

"The gods only know how soon they will be here in Dor," he said. "Egypt will not defend us. Her troops are needed at home, for the sea people have already set sail for the delta."

"The Egyptians gone," whispered his wife. "I have never known a time when they were not here. What will it be like without them?"

That night Ahmoses and I stood on the roof and watched the Egyptian garrison march quietly from the city. Many people watched them, silent and unmoving, no hatred and no liking in their eyes . . . nothing but wonder that, after four hundred years, they were finally gone.

"They will never come back," said Ahmoses. "It has happened at last. Egypt has lost the world." He spoke calmly, but I had never seen such a look of sorrow on his face.

"Will you go home?" I asked him.

He paused and frowned. Then a bitter, stubborn look that puzzled me, came into his eyes and he shook his head.

"What about you?" he asked. "Will you still go back to Tyre, now that the sea people are there?"

"Now, all the more," I answered. "I gave my promise."

« 22 »

The Scoundrel from Gaza

THE NEXT MORNING, very early, Elhanan called us and said that the ship of which he had told us had put into port. We took a hasty breakfast and made ready to depart.

There were tears in the eyes of the wife of Elhanan; and, before I could say goodbye, I had to swallow hard and wipe my eyes with the back of my hand. For I found that I had become very fond of these two people of Canaan; and, if things had been different, I would have liked nothing better than to stay and be as their son.

A two-tiered ship lay at anchor by the docks and we boarded her.

Before taking us to the cabin, under its awning, Elhanan gave us a warning.

"Say nothing," he said, "of having fought with the army of Sisera."

"Why not?" I asked, surprised.

"Because," said Elhanan. "The owner of the ship

is on board, and he would use it as an excuse to refuse us any favor. He calls himself an Israelite."

"Calls himself?"

"Yes. Of the tribe of Ephraim, he says. But he fears the Baals as well as any man, has traded in slaves stolen from the tribes, and only calls himself one of them when he thinks there is some profit to him. Though I do not like to say it of any man, he is a real scoundrel."

For some reason, his last words startled me, as if they should bring something to my mind. But what it was I could not remember.

The cabin to which we were taken was as roomy and handsome as the ones I had seen in the ships of Ethbaal. It was finer in fact, for it had hangings of Egyptian linen instead of goatskin. The owner of the ship sat at ease at the table, the master standing behind him. He reminded me of the rich robed, curled and ornamented man with the purse that we had seen on our first day in Dor.

Elhanan bowed low to him, his hands to his heart.

"Peace be with you Joash ben Omri. May your affairs prosper," he said.

"They have, Elhanan," said the man. In spite of the heavy, ornamented garments and the long curls and beard, I could see that he was tall and strong with a clever face and large, thinking eyes. There was something about his face that made me feel I had perhaps seen it before.

"Was the wind strong from Gaza?" Elhanan asked politely.

Then I had it. Gaza. Those scoundrels down in Gaza. And his eyes were the eyes of Jotham except that there were lines of greed and deceit around them. Surely this was the uncle, the Hebrew merchant from Gaza, who had stolen Jotham's birthright.

Elhanan told him of our plight, how we were penniless and bound for Tyre and how, because of the dangers of these uncertain times, we would prefer sea travel to venturing out overland.

I watched how Joash ben Omri was thinking that Elhanan was a good friend to have in the markets of Dor.

"It is only a day and half a night's sail to Tyre after all," he said at last. "It can do no harm to take the young men on if you take an interest in them. Though why you do," he added, looking at us rudely, "I do not understand."

Ahmoses and I did not care what he said. We had what we wanted and did not care how Joash insulted us out of his bad temper.

The bad temper seemed to be caused by something more than having to take on two poorly dressed passengers who couldn't pay for their passage; when Elhanan asked him how it was that he himself was sailing on this voyage, he flushed angrily.

"Must I have a reason to sail on my own ship?"

he asked. "It may be that I wanted to see for myself how I am being cheated by the Canaanites."

"*I* think," Ahmoses said to me later, "that it is because something frightened him down in Gaza."

"I wonder what it was," I replied cheerfully.

"With a man like him, it could have been anything. The Canaanites may have turned on him for being a Hebrew, or the Hebrews of the city may have threatened him for being a Canaanite. I suppose there are not many that he can trust."

I wanted to tell Ahmoses what I knew of Joash, but did not. I could not be sure it was the same man.

Night had fallen and we were lying in the open, against the bulwarks of the ship. This was my first sea voyage and, though we were always within sight of land, it was a wonderful thing to me. It was too dark now to see the shore, though far off in the distance I could hear the faint thunder of the surf. There were the stars right above me, clear and bright to guide us, holy with the names of the gods. And the movement of the deck beneath me was pleasant and soothing. I was not sick. Perhaps the buffeting I had had in the waters of the Kishon had cured me of that.

I lay on my back, my head on my arms. Now and then I turned my head to look at Ahmoses. In the light of the moon his face could be clearly seen. It looked odder than ever with its delicate nose and jutting jaw.

"Were you trained as a soldier?" I asked him.

"No," said Ahmoses. "Schoolboys in Egypt are not urged to make the army a career. Besides, my family was poor and could only send me to a charity school where we were all warned that the only way a poor boy could make his fortune was to become a scribe."

"You are a strange people, you Egyptians," I informed him. "It is strange to me that you could ever fight at all."

Ahmoses grinned. "We fought well enough to give you Hittites a good beating at Kadesh."

I sat up on my elbow. "What beating at Kadesh?" I asked hotly. "You and your Pharaoh Rameses were lucky to escape out of our hands with your lives. Every singer knows that story."

Ahmoses sighed. "What does it matter now," he said.

We sighted Tyre as the sun came up. I had never seen a city from the sea before, and I watched in delight as the sunlight glittered on its walls and on the ancient temple of Baal Melkarth on its sister island. But a stillness came over me when, for the first time, I saw the ships of the sea people in the harbor, lean ships with sharp prows for ramming.

"So we are here," said Ahmoses.

"Not yet awhile," said a voice behind us. It was Zimri the ship master. "*He* wants to see you."

There was an unpleasant look on his face. He followed us to the cabin amidships.

Joash ben Omri was waiting for us, looking at us

out of narrowed black eyes, his mouth grim and unsmiling. And he demanded that we pay him for the price of our passage.

"The price?" I repeated foolishly.

"Of course, the price," said Joash. "You have been a passenger on my ship. Passengers on my ship must pay their fares."

"There is no price!" I cried. "That was agreed between you and Elhanan."

"Agreed that there would be no price?" protested Joash, looking dumbfounded. "Never! I agreed to bring you to Tyre, and I have brought you. I never agreed to bring you for nothing."

I knew now why the trusting Elhanan had never become rich. I opened my mouth to call Joash a liar and a pirate, but Ahmoses interrupted me.

"Joash ben Omri," he said. "You know we have no money."

Joash shrugged and shook his head. "You know the law," he said.

I knew it too . . . that if we could not pay Joash, we must go into bondage to him. My heart began to pound dully. This was a new kind of fear.

"Suppose," said Ahmoses, "that we have a patron who is willing to pay our ransom?"

Joash looked hurt.

"Not ransom, young man. You took passage on my ship of your own free will. Your fare."

"Our fare, then," said Ahmoses obligingly. "How much is it?"

"Thirty silver shekels," said Joash sharply. "For each."

"Thirty silver shekels!" I shouted, my anger overcoming my fear. "That is the price of a ceremonial garment. It is the price of a war horse, the hire of a plough ox for almost three years!"

"Well," said Joash reasonably, "if your patron wants to barter a war horse or a purple robe . . ."

And I realized that our only chance of freedom lay in Ethbaal's willingness to ransom us. And, remembering what I had done to him and his family, I could not believe that he would.

"Direct me to your patron's house, and I will send a messenger," said Joash. Without hope, I gave him the directions, then turned aside in shame and sorrow.

"He does not know me," said Ahmoses, "so he will probably not redeem me. But if he sends the money for you, go. It would do me no good to have you in bondage too."

Joash ben Omri sat calmly at his big table, going over some accounts on a sheet of papyrus. I stared at the old pirate, hatred in my heart. They were scoundrels down in Gaza, indeed. And yet I knew that what he did was common among seamen and ship owners whether they sailed from Canaan, the ports of Egypt, or the islands over the seas. And, because these ships brought prosperity to their cities and their gods, all that they did was within the law and nothing could be done against them.

The messenger returned, and I hardened my heart to hear the bad news I was sure would come.

But another man was with him, and my heart leaped to see that it was Reuel, the butler in the house of Ethbaal.

"Reuel!" I cried. "He sent you! Then he has not turned against me."

"It was not he who sent me," began Reuel. But before he could finish, Joash cut in to ask him how much he had brought.

"Thirty shekels," said Reuel, "to redeem the young man Uriah-Tarhund, if it is he, and I see that it is."

Ahmoses had closed his eyes.

"Then only one is ransomed," said Joash shortly, forgetting the polite words "fare" and "passage." He counted out the silver with great care, then said, "The young man Uriah-Tarhund may go free."

I looked at Ahmoses and my heart turned over. Ahmoses, a slave at the oars of a Canaanite ship. Ahmoses who had twice saved my life. I remembered how he had said, "If you stay, I will stay."

I had an idea, but I knew it would only succeed if Joash were really the uncle of Jotham. It was my only chance. I spoke to Joash.

"Will you take him back with you to Gaza?" I asked him. "I would not if I were you."

Joash looked at me in astonishment, and some of the color left his face. Before he could stop himself, he had asked me what I meant.

"I mean," I said, "that there are many men of Israel

in Gaza. And Israel has made herself strong these past days. Or are you planning to stay in Tyre? I would not if I were you. Oh, you will get along well enough with the Philistines. But there are people in Tyre who might guess why you have left Gaza." I swallowed hard, for I was coming closer to my big gamble. "And there are people in Tyre who know something else about you, too."

I saw Zimri, the ship master, look at his employer and put his hand on his knife.

I said, "You would not dare kill me or take me prisoner now. My ransom has been paid; so if I do not return soon with Reuel, my patron will send men to look for me. The tide does not serve you, so you cannot get away till late in the day."

"Why should I want to keep you here when your passage has been paid?" asked Joash; but I thought that his voice trembled a little.

I drew a deep breath and offered a silent prayer. "Because I know who you are," I said. "I know something you have done."

Joash tried to smile. "I have done many things in a long life," he said. "What is this thing you think you know?"

"That you have robbed and cheated a man of your own people and, worse than all, of your own family."

"So you know that story," said Joash, and I could have shouted for triumph. "I tell you the men of Israel do not hold *that* against me. They thank me for opening their eyes to the evil in that son of a strange woman."

"You are wrong," I said, feeling a great joy for Jotham's sake. "Their eyes have been opened to the evil in *you.* Your kinsman returned to the tribes and was welcomed by them. Their chief, Barak ben Abinoam is as a father to him. Deborah the seeress herself has cast you out of the tribes. If you are given to them now, they will sacrifice you to their God."

All the color had left the face of Joash.

"That cannot be," he cried. "They drove him out."

"Would you like to be sent into the hills to find out for yourself?" I asked him. "The priests in Tyre will be glad to send you, once they know who you are and how you have insulted the Baals. Or perhaps they will spare you for a ransom . . . a very large one, much larger than thirty silver shekels."

"Who are you to threaten me in this manner?" cried Joash in a terrible voice.

"My patron," I said, "is that kinsman of Jotham ben Amram, who took him in after you robbed him of his birthright. He is a great man in Tyre. He will be glad to know your name and who you are."

Joash leaned back, looking sick. Suddenly I was ashamed; for he was a bold, clever man who looked a little like Jotham, and it could not have been easy for him to keep himself safe and make himself great in Canaan. It was not pleasant to see him looking beaten and frightened.

But I thought of the little boy Jotham, driven from his home and people. I thought of Ahmoses, tricked and trapped into slavery. And who knew what else he had done to make himself great, so that now all men were against him and there was no one to whom he could turn? I thought of these things and then I was glad to see that he looked afraid.

"If I were to say nothing about all this," I said, "my patron might let you go in peace."

A little smile hovered for a moment on the face of Joash.

"If I were to carry two passengers on my ship for one fare?" he asked. I nodded.

"The thirty shekels will redeem both you and your friend," he said shortly. "Now, both of you, get off my ship."

We made ready to obey. Then, puffed up as I was with success, another idea came to me and, before I could stop myself, I had spoken to Joash again.

"My patron will be more satisfied," I said, "if you will let me carry him some of the money you owe him."

"What money?" shouted Joash, rising in wrath, so that for the first time I quailed a little.

"The money he has spent for the keep of Jotham ben Amram, because you robbed Jotham of his birthright," I said, as firmly as I could. "Of course, Jotham has worked out some of it himself. I think sixty silver shekels would be enough."

There was a terrible silence and, for a moment, I knew an awful fear. Then Joash turned to Zimri.

"Give him the silver," he said heavily, and fell back into his chair, looking gray and old.

Zimri threw the silver on the deck at our feet. Ahmoses and I were not too proud to fall on our knees and gather it up, Reuel helping as best he could with his stiff joints. Then the three of us hastened from the cabin, down the gangplank and onto the great waterfront of Tyre, as if demons were following us.

"Did you once say," said Ahmoses, "that you would never make a trader? I think you would make the greatest trader I have ever seen."

My heart rejoiced. For I did not come to Tyre and the house of Ethbaal as a beggar; and I was sure now that I could take care of myself in this strange new world.

« 23 »

The New Masters

THERE WERE PHILISTINE soldiers in the streets of Tyre. They wore helmets crowned with plumes. The streets were quiet and, though the sun was shining, it was as if a shadow hung over the city.

Ethbaal was dead, Reuel had told me. He had died on the day that Tyre had opened her gates to the Philistines and had never heard the news I brought, the news of the death of Hannibaal. For this I was glad.

"If Ethbaal is dead," I asked Reuel, "who is it who paid my ransom?"

Reuel hesitated, looking scared.

"It was the mistress," he said at last, "the lady Merris. But you must not tell *him* that."

There was time to say no more; for we had come to the house of Ethbaal . . . the bright, shining, three-storied house that had taken my breath away when I had first seen it. It was like coming home, and I pushed my way through the great door and hastened to the common room, not stopping to have my hands and feet bathed. Ahmoses followed more slowly.

The common room was empty.

"Where is everybody?" I asked. Then, more soberly, I added, "Where are the lady Merris and the lady Mehitabel? And why are the servants so quiet?" For I had heard no laughter and not even a single voice.

"The ladies do not come to the common room now," said Reuel. "And the servants have no heart for gossiping. Besides, they are afraid."

"Afraid?"

But Reuel did not seem to want to say any more. "I will bring you some bread and cheese," he said. And he added, muttering to himself, "Even *he* would not have the face to starve a guest in the house."

He left the room but was back soon in the company of the little servant girl that I remembered so well, the one who played the flute. They brought a sumptuous midday meal of cheeses and greens and cakes and goat's milk. It seemed so natural and comforting to me to be served and hovered over again in the house of Ethbaal, that I began to forget the strangeness and the silence.

"Eat, Ahmoses," I said happily. "We are home and our troubles are over."

But, though Ahmoses smiled and ate, his eyes were sober and watchful.

Our meal was interrupted by the sound of a loud barking and snuffling outside in the courtyard. We heard the noise of scurrying feet as someone hastened to throw open the door; and a moment later two men walked into the common room.

One of them was Achil the Philistine. He was changed. He was dressed like a prince, his bronze hair sleek and curled on his shoulders, a patterned kilt of finest linen belted about his waist, fitted boots of the softest and thinnest leather upon his feet and precious ornaments upon his breast and arms. And he walked like the master of the house.

He stopped in surprise at seeing us there. Then he came toward us, the dog Pelops at his heels, a little smile on his face.

I rose to face him. And when he saw my face, the smile faded.

The little servant girl had come in to remove the dishes. She stopped still in fear, upon seeing who was there. Achil's eyes flickered over the table, then flashed an ugly look at the girl.

"You have been generous in my absence and without my leave," he said to her. Suddenly he raised his walking stick and swept the dishes from the low table onto the floor.

The girl turned pale.

"My lord," she quavered, "it was not my doing."

The second man stepped forward and spoke in a soft, mincing voice.

"What will it take to teach you," he said, "to be silent till you are told to speak?" The girl began to cry.

I stared at him. I remembered who he was . . . the slave Achil had given to the chief of Tyre. The slave that Jotham had said was not a slave but a spy. I turned to Achil in anger.

"Who is he," I said, "to speak in that manner to a servant in the house of Ethbaal? And who are you to come in like the master of the house, bringing your dog?"

"Who do you think is the master here, Uriah-Tarhund?" said Achil.

"Ethbaal is dead and Hannibaal too," I replied. "The master here is their nearest of kin, the nearest kin of the lady Mehitabel and the lady Merris."

"You have said it, Uriah-Tarhund," replied Achil, nodding gravely. "Therefore, I am the master here. For soon I will be their nearest of kin."

It came to me slowly.

"You are to marry Mehitabel," I muttered, not believing it. And then, in anger, I cried, "Who has given her to you?"

The slave who was not a slave spoke again in his peculiar, lisping accent.

"Lower your voice, barbarian. We Philistines are masters now in Tyre. We have only to take what we want. We need no permission from Canaanites."

I looked him up and down. There was a mean

triumph in his eyes. He was a slim, small man, darkly handsome, and carried himself straighter and prouder than any lord I had ever seen. He was surely of the ancient blood of the western islands, unmixed with the blood of the fair-haired northerners, a true heir of that great people. The northerners had conquered him, but now they had made him a conqueror again; and all the bitterness of the past was in his heart to make him vengeful and cruel.

"Deucalion is right," said Achil. "Still, I am not a savage. I am a man of Crete and there were ancestors of my mother who even served under Minos. I would marry no woman against her will or the will of her family. The lady Merris has given her to me."

"I don't believe it," I told him.

Achil nodded. "I see that you have hardened your heart against me, Uriah. You have learned the lesson of the Hittites badly. The lessons you will learn in Tyre will be more thorough, so I will give you some advice. Be out of this house, you and your friend, by tonight when I return."

Hearing the menace in his master's voice, the dog Pelops bared his teeth and growled softly. Achil took him by the collar and jerked him around. The three of them left the room, and we heard the outer door open and swing shut.

I stood in the center of the common room, staring at the broken dishes on the floor. I looked at Ahmoses. His face was very still.

Suddenly I clapped my hands hard.

"Reuel!" I shouted.

"I will bring him," said the little servant girl, who had stood trembling through it all.

"No, you can do it yourself," I said. "Go to the lady Merris and tell her that I am here. Ask her if I may come to her rooms."

« 24 »

The True King

THE LADY MERRIS sat alone in her parlor. She had not changed much since I had gone away. But her eyes were dim, and she no longer sat straight and proud in her chair.

I bowed before her and pressed her hands to my lips. Ahmoses stood in the shadows by the entrance.

"Good mother Merris," I said, "I have brought you sad news."

"My grandson," she said. "I knew when he left that he would not come back."

She closed her eyes and swayed back and forward. I thought she had forgotten I was there.

"Mother Merris," I said, "you have another grandchild."

"Out of all my children, only one grandchild left."

"You have another grandchild," I repeated, "one who has no one to turn to but you."

"Mehitabel," said the lady Merris. "But she is not mine now. I have given her away. She will be safe."

"You have given her to the evil one!" I cried.

"Do you know what the Philistines are doing in Canaan, what they will do in Egypt, the land of your birth? Do you know what they are doing here in this house?"

The lady Merris looked at me with puzzled eyes.

Ahmoses came to me and touched my arm. "Do not torment her," he said. "What can she do?"

At the strange voice the lady Merris looked up vaguely.

"Who is this you have brought here?" she asked me, a little of her old pride in her voice, offended at seeing a stranger in her rooms.

"A true friend," I replied. "A man of your own birth land. He is called Ahmoses."

Some of the dimness seemed to have gone from her eyes. She leaned forward, to see him closer.

"I have seen him before," she said.

"No, no, mother Merris. He has never been in Tyre and he was born long after you left Egypt."

To my amazement I saw that she had begun to tremble.

"But I have seen him before!" she cried.

I was frightened, for her very lips had begun to tremble and her eyes had become enormous in her thin old face. I turned to Ahmoses.

"Tell her," I urged him. "Tell her she could never have seen you before."

Then I stopped, amazed at the look on Ahmoses' face. He seemed to be trying to make up his mind whether or not to speak.

"It may be," he said at last, "that she has seen pictures or images of my family."

With all my troubles, I was almost ready to laugh.

"Your family!" I said impatiently. "A charity school boy does not have pictures or images of his family."

Ahmoses turned on me. I had never thought he could be angry, but now the fire of a great wrath burned in his eyes, and I started back.

"My family is the family of the last true kings of Egypt," he cried. "I am Pharaoh!"

A moment after, he lowered his eyes and flushed a little. And truly it was laughable for a penniless boy, an Egyptian mercenary in the outposts of Canaan to suddenly cry out that he was Pharaoh of Egypt.

But I did not laugh. I only said, somewhat feebly, "I don't understand."

Ahmoses raised his head and spoke with quiet pride.

"Smenkare himself, older brother of Tutankhamen, husband of Meritaton oldest daughter of the true Pharaoh, was my ancestor. I am the oldest son of all the oldest sons of the line. If the world were as it should be, I would be Pharaoh of Egypt."

I looked closely at his face, that I had always seemed to have seen before. Now I knew where it was I had seen it . . . in the little statue head of Nefertiti the Beautiful Lady, which now lay by the hand of the lady Merris. He was not beautiful, but he had the same delicate face and stubborn jaw.

For awhile the room was very still. And through my mind ran the stories I had heard of the ancient, legendary kings of Egypt, of the conquerors of Canaan, the builders of great cities, the accursed city of Akhetaton. They were gathered together in this boy who had fought beside me, lain on the ground at my side, and saved my life in the river.

"But why," I said at last, "are you not living as a great lord in Egypt?"

Ahmoses smiled.

"The men and women of my family live as peasants and exiles," he said. "Smenkare and Meritaton were murdered by the priests of the god Ammon, but their child was hidden away and Horemheb's men never discovered where. Only to that child's descendants was the story told, and we never tell it outside the family. I have told the story to no one but you."

The lady Merris was watching him with eyes that were no longer vague.

"The true king," she said. "Long ago I prayed to Aton that I might see the true king before I died. He has answered my prayer. It is a sign to me. I will commit no act of shame before him."

She turned commandingly to the little flute player. "Bring my granddaughter to me," she said.

Mehitabel came, and my jaw dropped at the sight of her. For she was dressed as I had never seen a woman dressed before, in a gown belted in jewels and her waist drawn in small as my hand. A golden skirt of many tiers swept the floor behind her; and I knew I was seeing a gown of the Cretan women, such a gown as they had worn to watch the bull dancing or in the great court of the House of the Double Axe.

But it was her face that stopped me short. It was as still and pale as Hannibaal's the night before he died. She did not look at me, but stood at the door stiff and still as a doll in her foreign gown; and I stepped back and did not try to greet her.

"I have a command to give you," said her grandmother.

"You have already given it," said Mehitabel gently. "I have told you that I will obey."

"This is a different command," said the grandmother quietly, and I saw Mehitabel frown in surprise at the change that had come over the old woman.

"When I told you I would give you to Achil," said the lady Merris, "you said you would obey me. But I knew it was not I whom you were obeying."

Mehitabel flushed suddenly and bowed her head.

"It was because Achil is strong," said the old lady, "and we are weak, and you thought you had no choice. But now I have another command for you, and you will obey it because I, the mother of your father, have given it."

She had risen from her chair with the aid of a stick, and now she brought the stick down hard on the floor.

"I forbid you to marry Achil," she said.

Mehitabel raised her head.

"You are right," she said. "I was not obeying you. I was obeying our new masters. And they are still our masters and they are still the ones I must obey, as Tyre has obeyed them. Like the city, I have no choice."

As if she had not heard her, the grandmother said, "Since you will now be in great danger in this house, I have another command. You will leave it, and you will leave the city. Tonight, before Achil returns."

Mehitabel's mouth fell open. She had turned pale again, but her eyes had come to life.

"What are you saying?" she cried.

The grandmother's voice trembled. "It is a hard thing I am telling you to do. Perhaps a terrible thing. But the other is worse, and there is always a choice." She looked at Ahmoses. "I have had a sign that has given me the strength to make it."

Ahmoses did not look much like a Pharaoh at that moment, and I could see he was not feeling like one either. But I gave him a warning look. He was the sign that would save Mehitabel, and it was up to him to be worthy of it.

"Where can I go?" said Mehitabel at last. Her eyes were frightened, but I saw that she too had made her choice. I spoke to her for the first time.

"Do you remember the story of the princess and the Hittite prince?" I asked her. "Do you remember what you said?"

Mehitabel looked at me with tears in her eyes.

"That if I had been that princess, and Jotham the Hittite prince . . . but Jotham is surely dead. He offended against Moloch."

"What if he is not?" I asked her. "What if his God is more powerful than Moloch and has protected him? You see that *I* am still alive. I cannot be sure about Jotham. But if he were alive, and heard about the Philistines in Tyre, he might come here to find you, and then he would surely die. Unless you went to him first."

"Where would he be?" she asked me.

"In Harosheth," I answered. "And that is where I must go too, to keep a promise."

"Take her with you," said the grandmother. "You are as my grandson and she is as your sister. And you," to Mehitabel, "go to your room and take off that devil's dress."

Suddenly Mehitabel began to laugh. She seized the old woman in her arms and covered her face with kisses. Then she ran from the room, the golden flounces clinking and rustling.

The lady Merris sank back into her chair. Ahmoses and I hastened to help her.

"It is a hard thing I have done," she whispered.

"I will take care of her," I promised. "I will be as her brother. And I am not such a fool as I was when I left Tyre. The ransom you sent for me this morning. Look, I have brought it back to you twice over." And I showed her the bag with the silver shekels.

"Keep it," said the old lady. "With my granddaughter in your charge, you will have earned it three times over before you are done. It is all I can give you or her, for Achil has taken our property."

"Come with us, mother Merris," I said, in sudden fear for her safety. But she shook her head.

"I am too old. I would be dead before you had me out of the city. I do not fear Achil, now that Aton has given me his sign."

She raised her hand and beckoned to Ahmoses.

"My king. My young king without a country. I have a tribute for you, the best I have to give."

She raised the little image of Queen Nefertiti in her hands.

"She was the mother of your line. I prayed that one day I might give her into the hands of the true king. She was the most beautiful of women and one day, when she was old, she gave this to a woman of my family . . ."

She fell silent, lost in dreams; and, though Ahmoses gave me the image to hold and bent to kiss her hands, I do not think she knew when we left the room.

« 25 »

Pelops

THE SUN WAS low when we were ready to leave. Mehitabel had made many preparations and gathered together many belongings; and, when I saw what she had, I told her she must leave them.

"But my jewels!" she cried. "Are people to take me for a slave? Besides, many of them are sacred. And how can I leave my household images? And what am I to do without my curling pins? And no one will know me without the paints for my mouth and eyes!"

"Jotham will know you, if he still lives," I replied firmly. "Do you want to draw down robbers? Besides, who do you think will carry them for you?"

"My porters," said Mehitabel grandly.

So I explained to her, as patiently as I could, that she could bring only one woman servant with her, and that we would have a hard time feeding that one; and that we had better save our strength for walking, not for carrying heavy bundles.

Mehitabel listened, frowning. But she was the

daughter of Ethbaal and could always understand good sense. She chose the little flute player to take along with her, Achil having sold away the old nurse whom she loved. The flute player wept for joy, being in such fear of Achil and his man, the Cretan Deucalion.

At last we were ready. The sun was down, and we were in a fever to be out of the house before Achil returned. And yet Mehitabel lingered in the hallway, looking about at the bright hangings and rich rugs, the dainty ornaments and colored tiles, with eyes full of tears.

"Come," I said to her. And I said, as my father had once said to me, "It is not your home. It is their home now."

At last we were in the street. And there, suddenly, Mehitabel stopped.

"Zebub!" she cried. She had turned very pale. "I had forgotten him."

Zebub was the Egyptian fox dog. She turned and I saw that she was ready to go back into the house.

"It is too late," I hissed at her. "Any minute now Achil will come around that corner with Deucalion, and then what?"

Mehitabel faced me, white and stubborn. "Achil will kill him," she said. "He will drown him, or set Pelops upon him. If you want to go without me, go. But I am going back for Zebub."

I could not let her go back. I had promised Hannibaal and the lady Merris.

"Wait here," I said. "Ahmoses, keep Mehitabel out of sight." And to Mehitabel I added bitterly, "And if I am slain in the house of your father, it will be on your head."

"You will find him on the roof, in the summer parlor," was all Mehitabel replied.

I moved as fast as I dared, yet silently too. For all I knew, Achil might already have come into the house. But I saw no one in the entryway or on the stairs; and I ran up them, leaping two at a time, so that I was breathless when I came to the roof.

Zebub, as Mehitabel had said, was in the summer parlor, snoring on a cushion. I seized him. He did not like to be wakened so rudely, and tried to bite me. I stuffed him under one arm and hastened out onto the open roof and toward the stairs.

"Barbarian!" shouted a voice behind me.

I whirled to face Achil, backed by his man Deucalion. They had been in the house after all, and had followed me up the stairs.

I dropped the little dog and waited for what would come. The two men came toward me.

"You did not listen to me. You came back," said Achil. "You came back to steal. A thief in the night may be slain with no questions asked. Deucalion!"

Moving faster than a snake, the Cretan got behind me and seized my arms. I stood as my father had once stood, pinned and helpless; and the blue-eyed man came toward me, balancing his stick in both hands.

But I was not my father. I was young and strong and well fed and, unlike him, I did not want to die. Besides this, I had learned things in my training outside Harosheth. And suddenly I bent and twisted, and the Cretan was no longer holding my arms but was lying flat on the roof. He had cracked his head on the stone. Whether or not he was dead, I did not know; but surely he would not hurt or frighten people for a long time to come.

Achil stood still a moment in amazement. And this gave me my chance to spring upon him and get hold of the stick. We wrestled for it, close together. I saw only his eyes . . . blazing blue eyes, the eyes of the man who had slain my father.

Suddenly the stick flew from our hands, clattering along toward the edge of the roof. I reeled from the surprise. Achil was still stronger than I. Before I could find my balance, he had borne me down on the stones. His hands were around my neck, his fingers digging into my throat.

There were red waves in the air before me. My head and my neck and my chest were bursting. But I could still see those blue eyes. I went for them with my thumbs. Over the roaring in my ears I heard him yell. The fingers loosened and grabbed my wrists; and the air, with great pain, rushed back into my chest. I rolled and twisted to get free of him, using my knees and feet. He fell away from me for a moment and I struggled up, holding onto the parapet at the edge of the roof.

In an instant he too was on his feet and coming upon me again. With a sickening fear, I knew what he would do, that he would force me over the edge.

I staggered away from the parapet. He sprang after me. And in that instant a brown body hurtled through the air, just missing me, and landing instead full upon the shoulders of Achil. I saw the Philistine reel and heard him scream; and then I saw him topple crazily over the edge and into the courtyard below. The dog Pelops stood, his forefeet resting on the parapet, and after a moment he began to howl.

Achil's shout had brought him. It was I he had meant to spring upon. For a moment I watched him in a kind of horror. Then, stepping over Deucalion who was breathing with a rasping sound, I gathered up Zebub who had watched it all with great interest, yapping with excitement. I tucked him again under my arm and, gasping the air back into me, ran down the stairs and into the street.

Ahmoses and Mehitabel and the flute player were waiting around the corner. Mehitabel's eyes widened when she saw me; but I thrust the fox dog into her arms and it was a long time before I would speak to her again, after all she had put me through.

"Achil is dead," said Ahmoses. He seemed to know things without being told.

I nodded. It was still hard for me to breathe.

"We must be out of the city before they find him," said Ahmoses.

We looked at Mehitabel. She was safe now from

the threat of Achil. Her wealth might keep her safe from those others of his kind. No one would accuse her of the murder of the Philistine. With us, who knew what might lie ahead?

Ahmoses too was thinking of this. He said to her, "Will you still come?"

She looked around her; and I knew she thought again of her gods and her possessions and the great, terrifying unknown that lay before her if she left them. But perhaps she thought of her kinsmen and her people and her priests bowing their heads before all those others like Achil. Perhaps she thought of all those children dead in useless sacrifice, and of her brother who had wanted to die. And I know she thought of Jotham.

She said, "I am coming."

We made our way to the city gate. The guard would have stopped and questioned us but a bar of silver quieted him. Soon we were out of the city, onto the causeway, and finally on the mainland itself.

I looked back at the walls of the town, gleaming pale in the moonlight.

Tyre will be a great city one day, I thought to myself. Greater than Sidon. She will never risk her treasures and the mighty and the powerful will always be her friends.

But I was glad that we had made a different choice.

« 26 »

Harosheth Again

THE HIGHWAY WAS crowded once more. But this time the caravans were different. Many of them were straggling bands of refugees from the north, where the sea people had been at their work of plunder and burning. The people were of all kinds, from slaves to princes. Some of them were richly dressed, and some had already walked their finery into rags. Some carried heavy bundles of possessions and clung to them still, though they would soon fall by the way from weariness.

When the sun rose, pink on the dust of the road, we fell in with a band of men and women and children from Sidon. From one man I bought a donkey for Mehitabel to ride. But the little flute player was so young and tired that Mehitabel put her on its back first a while to regain her strength. I was surprised, for she had never before given much thought to the feelings of slaves. Perhaps, I thought, it was because she had come close to being one herself.

The man had not wanted to sell his beast at first, but had finally agreed.

"Surely I have no use for silver on this road," he said. "Still it may be useful where we are going."

"Where are you going?"

"Into the hills," he replied. "As far from the coast as I can get."

"Have you not heard," I asked him, "that the cities in the hills have been taken by the tribesmen?"

The man shrugged hopelessly.

"Whoever they are," he said, "they can be no worse than the sea people." Suddenly his shoulders shook with sobs. "Sidon," he cried, "my beautiful Sidon, the queen of the seas! They have slain her elders and the Great One and have burned their houses. Their soldiers stand on the corners and cut down all who pass by, just for the sport. Why did we stand against them?"

Saddened, I left him to his grief. Then I saw that Ahmoses was standing by the side of the road, apart from the others.

"Hurry," I said to him. "We must keep up with the rest. Stragglers will only bring down thieves."

"I am not going with you," said Ahmoses.

I could not believe I had heard him right.

"I must leave you here," he said again. "You are going inland. I must take the road to the south."

"But why?" I protested. "The Philistines will be in all the coast cities soon. What is in the south?"

"Egypt," replied Ahmoses.

"Egypt?" I echoed. "You said you would never go back."

"Yes, I said that," said Ahmoses. "But have you ever been to the country near the mouth of the Nile? Have you ever gone fishing in the marshes in a little boat, or hunted in the reeds along the bank, or buried your feet in the black mud? You think Hattusas was a great city, or even Tyre. But have you ever been to Memphis? The avenues there are lined with trees and the images of the kings are as big as the greatest of Great Houses; and it is like hearing music to look out from a roof top, out across the gardens and the river toward the desert."

I looked at him helplessly, not knowing what to say.

"Let him go," said Mehitabel. "Adoni has called him back to Egypt. We must go where the gods lead us."

"You worship a god? You worship Adoni?" I asked him wonderingly. "I have never seen you bow before an image."

"The light of the sun is his image," said Ahmoses. "The sun shines on all men, even the Philistines, and so does Aton. But sometimes he must choose among them, and so must I. Sooner or later, the gods lead us home."

"How will you live along the way?" I asked him. And then I urged, "Divide the silver. It is half yours. Part of it was your ransom."

But Ahmoses shook his head.

"It was you who won it from the pirate," he said. "I have no need of it. Just give me my share of the food, to last me till I come up with some Egyptian garrison." He paused. "Will you not come with me? The Hebrews will be at Harosheth, but can you be sure Mehitabel's kinsman will be among them? And will they not kill you?"

It came to me that they very probably might. But I knew I must find out what had become of Sisera and his mother, for I had given my promise. And something else drew me toward Harosheth.

For a long time he and I looked at each other. I had first seen him only a moon or so before, yet I could not believe I would never see him again.

We embraced and I watched him out of sight down the highway, the true king of Egypt who had been the truest friend I had ever known.

"May your god be with you," I called after him; though I did not know why, for I no longer worshipped any gods.

And so, with the footsore band of Sidonians, Mehitabel and the flute player and I continued on toward Harosheth. In the middle of the second day we came upon it, and I saw the dark walls as I had seen them for the first time that day when I had been dragged along by the Canaanite soldiers with a rope around my neck.

But today smoke rose from within those walls. And I knew that Harosheth had been taken and put to the torch.

Outside the smoking walls was a great encampment. I caught my breath to see it, for it seemed that it must be the encampment of Sisera where I had trained and had ridden Labarnash. There were the fine tents of the captains of a thousand that I had envied so, and, towering above the rest, the many colored tent of Sisera. Chariots were ranged beneath an awning and horses tethered in a compound. I felt as if I were in a dream.

But when we came closer I saw that the masters of these tents and chariots were not the smart captains and well-trained troops of Canaan. They were a strange mingling of men and women and children, of all kinds, from sober herdsmen and craftsmen to proud chiefs and fierce-eyed savages. They were clothed in all manner of garments, from rags to shining, captured Canaanite breastplates and linens.

They came to stare at us when we came in sight, and to listen in wonder to the tale of the Sidonians. They gave us leave to camp not far from their tents. They traded food to the Sidonians in return for silver and fine garments and precious ornaments; and it was strange to look upon rough bearded, half-naked men now weighted down with jeweled pendants or gleaming arm bands, while the former owners gnawed eagerly on a hunk of bread or an onion.

An old woman let us share her tent; and Mehitabel, who had never waited on anyone before, now set herself to carry water and start a fire. I was amazed at how well she did. The little flute player was far slower at it than her mistress. But I could see that the eyes of the Canaanite girl were perplexed and frightened at their first glimpse of this new life and a great misgiving came over me.

"What have I done?" I thought. "To what have I brought her? Would Hannibaal thank me for this?"

I left the tent and looked out to the camp of the Hebrews. My flesh crept at the thought of making myself known to them.

"Will they not kill you?" Ahmoses had said.

Some children of the tribesmen had come in curiosity to poke about the camp of the Sidonians. One of them, a brown, tough-looking little fellow, had seen me and was staring at me with solemn eyes. He came toward me slowly.

"Uriah-Tarhund," he said.

"How do you know my name?" I asked him. Then I saw who it was. It was Jabin, the pale, perfumed little lamb of Moloch that I had first seen, glittering with ornaments, on the waterfront at Tyre. Now he was roughly clad and hard and sure on his feet, and might have been a different child altogether.

I put my hands on his shoulders and arms, to feel his muscles, and ran them over his curly hair.

"They have fed you well enough," I said. "Have they treated you well too?"

"They are good to me, as no one before," said

Jabin. "They let me go out with the sheep and play with the animals; and they have taught me to use a sling and a stone, and Tamar tells me stories."

My heart jumped. "Is Tamar well?" I asked him.

"She is well," said Jabin. "But she doesn't smile much, and she never talks of you."

His eyes were sober still and, I thought, a little scared. I drew in my breath and asked the question I had been afraid of.

"Did Jotham ben Amram live through the battle?"

His eyes brightened.

"Yes, and he is a hero," he said proudly. "He killed the black man, the charioteer of Sisera. And he would have slain Sisera himself. But when Sisera saw that the black man was dead, he turned coward and came down from his chariot and ran."

"What became of him?" I asked, with a heavy heart.

"They say he is dead, but I am not sure how. And before they burned the city, they went to the Great House to save his mother for she was an old woman. But she was gone. Some say the slaves rose up and killed her, but some say she was slipped out of the city and taken to Carchemish, the Hittite town in Amor."

I hoped that this last was true. In any case, I was freed of my promise concerning her. And now I turned my mind to the other thing I had to do.

I said to Jabin, "Go to Jotham ben Amram. Tell

him that I am here. Tell him that I have brought him a gift."

The scared look came back to Jabin's eyes.

"Must I tell him?" he said. "They say you are an enemy of Israel. I would not like to see you killed, Uriah-Tarhund."

"Jotham will not kill me," I said. Somehow I was sure of that. "Give him my message, Jabin. He will thank you for it."

After Jabin had left, I stood a while outside the tent. The other Hebrew children lingered about and I saw them whispering and giggling and pointing toward me. One of them came forward, pushed by the others.

"Are you a Sidonian?" he whispered.

"No," I replied.

"But you are an enemy of our God!" called out another from in back of the group. They all giggled nervously.

"I am an enemy of no god," I assured them.

"Our God is the enemy of all the others," said one, boldly. "And He has overthrown them."

"Where is He, your God?" I asked them.

"There, on that high place, in that tent that is finer even than the tent of Sisera," said the first child. "They brought Him up to be with us in the battle."

I looked where he pointed. It was indeed a mighty tabernacle that stood on a hill outside the camp.

"I would like to see Him," I said suddenly.

"You cannot see Him," said the child, looking shocked. "He lives in a wooden box covered with gold. They call it the Ark of the Covenant and no one may touch it on pain of being cursed."

I could not take my eyes from the tent. Their God was in there. He had sent Deborah her visions, and the rains that had destroyed the army of Sisera. The image must be in the box, I told myself. I would like to see it.

We sat that night, the old woman, Mehitabel, the flute player and I, about the common dish in the tent. Mehitabel's eyes were upon me throughout the meal, with sober questioning, but I could not bring myself to meet them.

Toward the end of the evening I heard steps outside the tent. I sprang to my feet, meaning to meet him outside. But then I saw Mehitabel's face, pale and scared, saw that she had already guessed who it was and that she was as fearful as I was.

He pushed through the opening of the tent and stood in the fire light in gleaming, captured armor, his hair falling rough and untended about his sun darkened face. His feet were bound with rags, his hands hardened and rough. Never again would I think it strange to see him, a lord of Tyre, in the tents of the shepherds. He was wholly a tribesman now. My heart sank for Mehitabel's sake.

His eyes were upon me, dark and angry. Then suddenly they changed and a look of wonder, almost of fear, came into them; for Mehitabel had risen behind me, and he had seen her.

I saw him look down at his rough clothes and broken fingernails, saw him smooth back his hair with a humble, frightened gesture and raise his eyes fearfully to hers. I saw the color come back to her face and saw her smile. Then they moved, faster than I would have thought possible, and their hands were clasped together as if nothing could ever loosen them. Neither of them looked at me again.

I made up my mind. I would not spoil this happiness I had given them. I would put no burden of choice concerning my life or death on Jotham's shoulders. When I walked out of the tent, they did not even see me go.

« 27 »

The Ark of the Covenant

I WALKED THROUGH the makeshift tents of the Sidonian refugees. Some of them did not even have tents, but huddled about fires in the open. The man who had sold me the donkey called to me as I passed.

"Where are you going, Uriah-Tarhund?"

"To the chief of the tribesmen," I answered him.

"Don't go!" cried the man.

But I walked on. The great tent of Sisera was before my eyes, and I knew who must be within it. I remembered his voice above the battle, when I had lain across the body of Labarnash; and how, even then, it had cleared my mind and cooled my fever so that I could rise to my feet again. There is no one left for me to go to but him, I thought. I will not hide from him.

Two soldiers stopped me when I came to the Hebrew camp.

"I must see the chief," I said to them.

"Why should we take you to him?" said one of them. "How do we know you are not an enemy?"

"I am an enemy," I replied. "I fought against you in the battle on the plain."

They stared at me as at a madman.

"Here," I said. "You see I have no weapon."

"Do you want to die?" asked the other soldier.

"I only want to see Barak," I replied.

They looked at each other, and finally the first one shrugged.

"Let him have his wish," he said grimly.

They took me through the camp, through braying pack animals and barking dogs, through men telling stories and playing games around fires. Some of them were singing, and I heard snatches of the song:

"The kings came and fought,
Then fought the kings of Canaan
In Taanach, by the waters of Megiddo . . .
The stars in their courses fought against Sisera.
The river of Kishon swept them away,
That ancient river, the river Kishon . . .
Awake, awake Deborah;
Awake, utter a song:
Arise Barak, thou son of Abinoam . . ."

We came to the tent of Sisera. A sentry listened to the whispered words of the two soldiers, stared at me a moment, then went inside. In a moment he was back and pointed me silently inside.

I felt as in a dream, as if I were back in time, going in with Memnet to worship again with Sisera before the image of the thunder god. I forced my feet to move and they carried me, blinking, into the light of torches.

There was no more image of Teshub, and no more image of blue-headed Dagon. The rich ornaments and furnishings were gone, parceled out probably among the heroes of the battle. There was only a rug and a brazier of coals, and Barak on his camp stool. He was alone.

I looked at him, the simple herdsman, the great warrior. He looked tired beyond belief, and stared at me with puzzled eyes. His beard was ragged and his arms were bare. But he wore a shimmering breast plate that I remembered well; and in that moment I knew for sure that Sisera was dead.

"Why did you come here?" he asked me.

"To keep a promise," I answered. "Besides, I had nowhere else to go. The Philistines are on the coast."

"You might have stayed with them," he said, his eyes searching my face.

I shook my head. "I could not."

He bowed his head and closed his eyes, and I knew he wanted sleep more than anything else. But I had given myself into his hands and felt that I could ask him a favor.

"Before you pass judgment on me," I said, "tell me how Sisera died." For I wanted to hear it from his mouth and no other. He, I knew, would not mock.

Barak sighed and spoke heavily.

"He fled north from the plain, and we pursued him. He came to the tents of Heber the Kenite, who had told him our secrets. The woman Jael was there, whom his soldiers stole from her family when she was a child."

I remembered the still face of Jael and her strange eyes. My skin crept.

"She called him into her tent and made him welcome; and when she saw him weak from hunger and thirst, she gave him goat's milk instead of water, and cheese in her finest bowl. Then, while he slept, she came to him and killed him, with a tent pin and a hammer. She struck off his head and gave it into my hands. Listen. They sing of it now."

Outside the tent I heard the high voice of a singer.

"Blessed among women shall Jael be,
The wife of Heber the Kenite . . .
He asked water, and she gave him milk;
She brought forth butter in a lordly dish . . .
At her feet he bowed, he fell, he lay down:
At her feet he bowed, he fell:
Where he bowed, there he fell down dead."

Memnet had not been there to guard him, and a woman had had the glory of his death. Memnet had been right to say that he feared all the people; and he had been right to fear them, for they had suffered greatly at his hands. Yet he had loved my father and been good to me, and I mourned his death.

I rubbed the tears from my cheeks, and raised my eyes to Barak, waiting for his judgment.

"It was Heber the Kenite who betrayed us," he said, looking hard at me. "He has been given to our God."

I flushed with shame. Yet it was true. I had told Sisera nothing he had not known from Heber.

"I am sick of death," said Barak. "What gods do you worship?"

"I don't know," I confessed.

"Can you find it in your heart to worship the one God of Israel?"

"I don't know," I said again.

"Find out," said Barak. "If you can, stay. Otherwise, go down to Egypt and bow before idols with the heads of beasts. Or go back to Tyre and cringe to the Philistines and let your children be devoured by Moloch. But do not play us false again, or you will surely die."

I stood again beneath the stars, wandering without purpose through the camp of the tribesmen. Outside, on a high place, was the tabernacle that the child had said housed the God of Israel. I will see Him, I told myself. Perhaps He will give me a sign. And I hurried through the darkness, stumbling sometimes in my eagerness to climb the hill.

A young man lay outside the tent to guard it. He looked like a priest of Egypt, for he was dressed in linen and his head and face were shaven. It was strange to see such a man among these people; but I remembered the stories of Deborah and the many years of their strange history.

"I have come to see your God," I told him.

"No one but the priests can enter here," said the young man. "But I will hold back the entrance, and you can look in."

In strange expectation, I looked inside. The tent was lit by a golden candlestick with seven branches. The light fell upon an object that looked like a great box, carved from a solid block of wood, covered with gold, and with gold rings through which staves were passed. On either side, looking toward the center were two cherubim with the wings and heads of eagles.

"Is your God in there?" I asked the priest.

He shook his head.

"The Ark of the Covenant holds relics sacred to our God. Some say they are the tablets with the laws that He gave to our great leader, Moses. No one knows."

"And there is no image of Him?"

"How could any man," said the young priest, "make such an image?"

I turned away, a great disappointment in my heart. I could not see Him after all. He would give me no sign. He, too, had failed me.

But as I walked back to the camp, I looked at the moon and the stars. They are gods, they had told me. But I no longer believed it. And if they and the sun and the earth and the sea and the rivers were not gods, what God had made them? And who, indeed, could picture such a One as that?

"How manifold are Thy works," Ahmoses had sung, "oh sole God like Whom there is no other."

And I decided that I did not have to see Him, and that He did not have to send me a sign. And I knew what it was that had led me again to Harosheth.

« 28 »

Home

HAROSHETH HAD FALLEN, and Taanach. And not long after runners brought word that the great city of Megiddo had been starved into surrender. The greatest towns of inland Canaan were in the hands of the tribes. The Ark of the Covenant was carried by the priests in triumph to the sacred town of Shiloh in the south; and many pilgrims followed it, singing the new Song of Deborah:

"Awake, awake, Deborah;
Awake, awake, utter a song:
Arise Barak, and lead thy captivity captive
Thou son of Abinoam . . ."

I had hoped to see Deborah herself again. But she had returned to her home after the battle on the plain. She had been with them there and had offered her life with theirs. But now, she said, they had no more need of her; and she, being old and tired, had much need of rest.

It was Jotham who told me this. He had come and asked me for Mehitabel. There was no one else to ask, and I had made myself as her brother.

"I have no bride price," he warned me.

"Yes you have," I said, suddenly remembering one of the things I had meant to tell him. "Your uncle has fled from Gaza and the south of Canaan. You have only to go to your home and claim your property."

I told him the story of the sea voyage and the ransom and we both laughed aloud, though it had surely not been funny at the time. And Jotham promised to pay me the bride price, in silver or in cattle, whichever I chose.

On a day not long after, he came to our tent to lead the veiled Mehitabel to the wedding feast. He shone and jingled with wedding ornaments, captured on the field of battle, and was accompanied by friends. One of the friends was Samuel, the son of Hushai.

I had not seen any of the family of Hushai since I had come to the encampment of the Hebrews. I had not looked forward to facing them, for I could not forget how I had betrayed their hospitality. And Samuel, who had hated me anyway, was the last one I had wanted to see.

He paused a moment at the sight of me; and I stood back, away from the joking and the laughter, not knowing what to do or say. Then he came toward me.

"If he wants a fight," I thought to myself, "I can

do nothing but face him. But my heart will not be in it."

We looked at each other for a moment. Then, suddenly, he laid his hand on my shoulder.

"Why do you hang back?" he said. "The feast is in the tent of my father, and you are the giver of the bride."

And then I saw that if Jotham and I had been changed by the battle on the plain, so had he. Probably in that one day he had seen enough men slain before his God to last his lifetime. He looked older and sadder, and there was no more hatred in his eyes.

So, with no more misgivings, I joined the wedding party and danced and clapped my hands with the rest on the way to the feast, listening to the wedding songs.

And at the wedding feast I saw Tamar again. She did not speak to me or meet my eyes. But she passed the wine cup; and when she gave it to me I set it down and took hold of her hands. They were locked together as Jotham's and Mehitabel's had been in the tent of the old woman, and I knew at last that I had come home.

That was many years ago. The tents of the Hebrew camp have long been scattered, and only birds and animals wander in the ruins of the great city of Harosheth. However, Megiddo was not destroyed, and has become a strong fortress city for Israel as it was for Canaan.

Canaan has new lords now. Israel is strong in the hills and the hand of the Philistines is heavy on the coast; and, like Canaan, all the world around us is changing masters.

The sea people did not conquer Egypt. But they broke her power and took her lands and the world will never again tremble at her name.

We look to the north and to the west now. North, to those rough heirs of the old Babylonian power, the Assyrians, who cast greedy eyes on the world that was lost by the Hittites; and to the mountains of the northeast, whence stories come of fierce Median and Persian tribes that hover on the edge of the known world and wait their chance to come down. West, to the little known lands across the sea that sent us the sea people, and that now mutter and rumble among themselves like wakening giants. The shadow of the future is theirs, not Egypt's.

But for the present we wait only for the day when the Philistines will come upon us, mightier than the Canaanites ever were, and we know that day will come soon. And over the tribes, from the east, hangs always the shadow of the desert people . . . Amelek, Moab, Midian . . . so that Israel is beset by many enemies. But the hills are on her side and so is her God, and the memory of Deborah and Barak gives her strength.

For my story: I married Tamar. I have a son and three daughters. I am old, and Jotham and Mehitabel are old; and Jabin, who has become a strong man among the tribes, has hair and a beard that have already turned gray. We live as neighbors not far from the sacred town of Shiloh, within sight of the tabernacle that houses the Ark of the Covenant.

I became a scribe. Who would have believed it in the days when I rode the steppes of Arzawa and jeered at all men who could read and write?

But such men were much needed in Shiloh; and, looking into my heart, I knew it was the life I had been born for, though I would never have known it if the sea people had not taken Great Hatti. I have devoted my life to my new God, whom I have come to believe is the one God and the God of all men. I have travelled much, collecting and writing down the ancient songs and stories that are sung of Him. The prophecies too, and one that is most dear to me: the prophecy of a Lord of Lords, who will one day be born to bring His message to all the nations of the world. Perhaps, in dark days that will surely come upon us, such writings will be destroyed; but may they never be forgotten.

In this manner I live, and I have prospered too. Outside the city I have flocks and herds. Even horses, bred from one of those that were taken after the battle on the plain. One of them belongs to my grandson . . . a long eared, golden horse that he raised and trained from the day of its birth, and was the first to harness. He calls him Labarnash.

About the Author

JOANNE S. WILLIAMSON was born in 1926, in Arlington, Massachusetts. Though she had interests in both writing and music, and attended Barnard College and Diller Quaile School of Music, it was writing which became the primary focus for her career after college. She was a feature writer for Connecticut newspapers until 1956, when she moved to Kennebunkport, Maine and began to write historical fiction for children.

In all she wrote seven such novels, each one exploring unusual historical slants of well-known events. In her first book, *Jacobin's Daughter,* she tells a true story of the French Revolution; in *The Eagles Have Flown,* she presents a picture of Julius Caesar's time and gives a sympathetic portrayal of Brutus. She has a remarkable knack for using her fictional characters and plot to make connections between real historical persons and events. In a time when history is often taught in bits and pieces these connections are a great help, not only to the younger reader, but to the older one as well. Her third book, *Hittite Warrior,* is an exceptional example of this facility for showing the inter-relatedness of ancient peoples and events and in making them come alive.

Commenting on *Hittite Warrior*, Miss Williamson says: "As a child I loved the old Bible stories in which the Hittites kept cropping up, and used to wonder who they were and where they came from. Later, when I was searching for a theme for my third novel, I remembered my old curiosity and decided to satisfy it. What I discovered in the archaeological source materials led to the creation of the young warrior Uriah and his adventures in a crucial era of Bible history."

Her last book, *To Dream Upon a Crown*, a retelling of Shakespeare's Henry VI trilogy, was published in 1967, coinciding with the unfortunate decline in America of interest in intelligent historical fiction for children. Miss Williamson then returned to her second calling and taught music until her retirement in 1990. It is to be hoped that in the reprinting of *Hittite Warrior* the author's fascination with history will kindle an answering spark in a whole new generation of children, which in turn will affect both the living and the writing of the history of the future. Joanne Williamson died July 5, 2002.